The Outlaws of Salty's Notch

The elderly derelicts in the sleepy Louisiana settlement of La Belle Commune are leading the good life, lazing in the hot sun. Until Bushwhack Jack Breaker rides in from Texas with his outlaw band, and everything changes. Ex-bounty-hunter Paladin awakes to find eccentric marshal, Brad Corrigan, has been forcibly taken, along with saloonist Rik Paulson and storekeeper Alec Mackie – but where, and why? The elegant widow Emma Bowman-Laing knows where, but Paladin and crippled wrangler Shorty Long fail in their rescue bid and Bowman-Laing's crumbling antebellum mansion goes up in flames.

With rumours of a horde of gold coming across the sea by ketch, and flashy Mexican killer Guillermo Rodriguez brandishing his six-gun, Paladin slips reluctantly into his old bounty-hunting ways. His search for truth and justice takes him deep into Texas, but it is in La Belle Commune that everything is resolved in a bloody fight in the saloon, and brought to a fatal close in the waters of Petit Creek.

D1357456

The Outlaws of Salty's Notch

Will Keen

A Black Horse Western

ROBERT HALE · LONDON

ISBN 978-0-7198-1420-4

Robert Hale Limited
Clerkenwell House
Clerkenwell Green
London EC1R 0HT

www.halebooks.com

Typeset by
Derek Doyle & Associates, Shaw Heath
Printed and bound in Great Britain by
CPI Antony Rowe, Chippenham and Eastbourne

PART ONE

ONE

The rider on the blue roan was halfway through the town of La Belle Commune when Paladin, beer-glass in hand, picked his way unsteadily across the rotting timber gallery outside Paulson's Place. The stranger, a raw-boned moustachioed man armed with six-gun and rifle and wearing a flat-crowned black hat grey with trail dust, was drawing level with the shack that served as the town's jail. Walking his horse without haste, he was alert, watchful, his head constantly turning. A glance took in the store. Another the saloon. An ironic grimace twisted his lips as sharp eyes took careful note of the drab surroundings.

La Belle Commune's single street was little more than a wide expanse of bone-dry earth, stony and rutted. Single-storey buildings were sagging beneath the unrelenting Louisiana heat, their woodwork eaten by termites and bleached white by the merciless sun. A general store, the saloon with wide shaded gallery where Paladin stood watching, the jail that looked a tarted-up chicken coop, a scattering of dwellings trailing away into the shimmering distance – La Belle Commune was as impressive as a dried out waterhole, a Louisiana settlement close to the Texas border sinking into senility.

Then the rider's eagle gaze alighted on the side trail that ran alongside Mackie's store, cut through a low sandy ridge and sloped lazily south for a hundred yards to the ocean where palm trees lining the beach drooped listless green fronds against the endless blue skies over the gulf.

Something about that side track seemed to please him, Paladin noted. The man smiled, nodded to himself and sat straighter in the saddle as he heeled his horse to a faster pace and headed east out of town. That trail would take him, Paladin mused, half-a-mile or so to the timber bridge affording a crossing of Petit Creek – and then where?

The stranger had been watched all the way by Brad Corrigan. Brad was sitting outside the jail in his rocking chair. Smoke from the cigarette in his lean hand rose straight and thin in the hot, still air. The slow creaking of his chair was no match for the fading beat of the departing horse's hoofs, and the mid-afternoon sun struggled to pick highlights from his tarnished badge. In that dazzling sunlight La Belle Commune's marshal seemed half asleep. His battered Derby hat was perched on hair like dry hay. Sweat-stained and mildewed green with age, it was tipped forward, shading his eyes. Beneath its curled brim those pale blue eyes appeared remote, uninterested.

And that was deceptive, Paladin thought. Brad sees him all right, files him away mentally just as I do – and with good reason. As he leaned on the gallery's shiny wooden rail and swallowed the last of his warm beer, Paladin recalled the other riders who had passed through La Belle Commune. Four in as many days – some kind of a record.

One a young half-breed or full Mex', but Texas gunmen every one of them: dusty, hard-eyed, watchful, armed with six-guns and rifles, blued metalwork tarnished, stocks and butts glossy from constant handling. To believe there was nothing connecting them with the moustachioed rider whose dust was a drifting haze in the sunlight would be foolish; to fathom that connection was too much for a man whose mind was rusty with disuse, halfway to addled by heat and strong drink.

Which, Paladin thought wryly, led to the obvious question: why the hell was he getting his pants in a twist? La Belle Commune was a lazy settlement on the Gulf of Mexico's palm-fringed Louisiana coast, with a population counted on the fingers of two hands. Any money that jingled on the hardwood counters of the store, or on the rough planks that served the same purpose in the saloon, was earned by a handful of old fishermen, and no-hopers who worked on odd jobs further inland. Saw enough wood, hammer in enough nails to earn a pocketful of silver dollars. Laze away the next few days or weeks in town, where salt-laden onshore evening breezes cooled the air and rattled fronds of skeletal palm trees. Jingle coins on the bar in Paulson's Place. Awake one day to poke a hand deep into a pocket, encounter nothing but dust, reluctantly ride north to find work.

Paladin was spared even that minor irritation. He had earned his money in a way he never specified but from which he bore mental and physical scars that were testimony to its ugliness and its dangers. He'd been a hard man, in an occupation that had no place reserved for morals or conscience. And as he gingerly negotiated the rickety steps and set off across the settlement's baking thoroughfare, he reflected yet again on a fact that was strangely comforting: shrewd Brad Corrigan had watched his arrival in town some two years back, and from that first day could read him like an open book.

Paladin, as he would himself admit in the lonely hours of the long nights, was a spent force. A shadow of the man he had once been, all the decisiveness and lightning-fast reactions in explosive, dangerous situations long since gone. He drank too much, lived in a world of brooding melancholy.

The marshal watched Paladin's approach, shifted his weight in the chair so that it creaked in protest. He dropped a hand, let go his cigarette and crushed it beneath one of the rockers. By the time Paladin had come around the hitch rail he was up on his feet, a man of extraordinary height and as thin as a beanpole.

'That makes five,' the marshal said.

Paladin nodded. 'You want my opinion? I'd say that's an end to it. The others were as nothing compared to that *hombre*. He was one mean sonofabitch, a man not to be crossed.'

'A leader,' Corrigan agreed, and he swung away and ducked through the door into the cooler shadowy interior of the office. 'A *honcho*,' he elaborated as Paladin followed and dropped into a battered chair, 'but a *honcho*'s a boss man – so what is it that feller's bossing? If we had a bank I'd say he was here to beat that raggedy bunch that preceded him into some kind of shape to stage a robbery. But the nearest bank is fifty miles to the east. What in the name of God are those hellions doing, here, in the middle of nowhere?'

'Always supposing,' Paladin said, 'all five of them haven't

ridden straight on through, put La Belle Commune well behind them and are halfway to Baton Rouge.'

'But you don't think that any more than I do,' Corrigan said, folding his length into his swivel chair and slapping his hat on the desk. 'Like me, you saw him eyeing Salty's Notch. So what the hell was all that about?'

An inner door was open. Beyond it, out of sight, an open window by the empty cell was providing a through draft. Paladin whisked off his hat, relished the feel of cool air on his damp forehead, musing on the marshal's words.

Some fifty years back an old fisherman had used a skinny mule to drag his flat bottomed skiff from his hut to the shore and into the sea. Day after day. There and back. Over time, that use had worn a deep, wide groove in the soft sandy earth of the low ridge that lay between town and sea. Salty Logan was long gone, as was the stubborn mule. But others had made use of the opening he had created, and his legacy was the broad track leading down to the shore that was known as Salty's Notch. Which, Paladin agreed, had been of inordinate interest to the hard-eyed horseman.

'Only thing a man finds down the notch,' he said, 'is sand and the big wide ocean.'

'So we've got five Texas gunmen taking a vacation from holding up stage coaches or trains, drinking warm beer under palm trees too tall and dried out to offer shade. Why would they do that?'

'Waiting,' Paladin suggested.

'For their boat to come in?'

'To La Belle Commune? Hah. There's a couple of flat bottomed skiffs owned by old fisherman trawling with rotting nets. Any other boats out there, hell, they're

11

making for New Orleans, giving this place a wide berth if they see it at all.'

Corrigan was nodding. 'Maybe,' he said, 'this place's anonymity makes it attractive to somebody out there in a way we don't understand.'

'And never will.'

'I guess so,' Corrigan said. 'But setting aside my weak jokes about palm trees and warm beer, we're left with five gunmen who came riding out of Texas for a reason. It might be interesting to find out where they are now, and what the hell it is they've got planned.'

At that moment Alec Mackie came in through the street door. He owned the store across the street next to Paulson's Place where Paladin roomed. He was a middle-aged burly character with a florid face and bright blue eyes. His wife had left him in Laramie, and he'd spent a year drifting south with cash in the bank and his eyes full of emptiness. If La Belle Commune had a town council, Mackie was one-third of it. He liked to call himself the town mayor, but did it with sadness in those blue eyes put there by the conviction that everyone in La Belle Commune was living proof that life was cruel.

'Whatever it is,' the storekeeper said, letting Paladin and the marshal know he'd caught Corrigan's drift, 'it's surely beyond my comprehension. Five gunmen descending on La Belle Commune with, what, an eye to making a heap of money? Don't make me laugh.'

'My past experiences in north Texas cow towns makes me unfailingly suspicious, Mac,' Corrigan said.

'Suspicion's all right, in its place,' Mackie said, leaning back against the windowsill, 'but that place ain't La Belle

Commune. You want my opinion, you're creating a gang out of five total strangers who're long gone. And you're doing it because you're two intelligent men who've had too little to do for far too long.'

But Brad Corrigan was having none of it.

'I stayed alive by seeing evil in any disreputable characters I met until they proved me wrong. My guess is around this same time tomorrow morning the widow Bowman-Laing'll come walking daintily down the street under her broken-ribbed yellow parasol. If we saw those fellers passing through town, you can bet your boots that old gal's sharp eyes tracked 'em a good part of the rest of the way, and in that perky, bright-as-a-button way she has she'll give us something to chew on.'

'Always supposing,' Paladin said with a grin, 'that like Mac says we're not just just a couple of over-excited old-timers talking through our hats.'

'You're not,' said a firm voice from the doorway.

The widow Emma Bowman-Laing had appeared sooner than expected. Tall, slim, elegant, her blonde-grey hair was coiled in a neat chignon. A faded, washed-out cotton dress hung from bony shoulders and brushed her sandals. The parasol she used to protect her ageing skin from the sun was folded, one rib poking through the fabric like a broken fish bone.

'That's reassuring,' Corrigan said, 'and I'm sure you're going to tell us why you think that, Emma.'

'Not think, know. I was up by my old house in almost pure darkness a couple of weeks ago. You know I ride there most nights?'

'That's where your memories lie,' Corrigan said. 'It

13

would surprise me if you could stay away.'

'Yes, well, for some years now you've known what I think about that,' Bowman-Laing said.

'And you know,' Corrigan said, 'that one day, soon as it's possible, we're going to do something decisive, set the record straight, roll back the years.'

For a moment there was silence. Then Emma Bowman-Laing sighed.

'I rode across the slope, close to the lawns, keeping my eyes averted because I know how a glimmer of light catches them. But I saw him, on the top balcony, and he wasn't too clever. Stepped back, but the glow of a cigarette betrayed him.'

Corrigan pursed his lips. 'The place is old and empty, Emma. Weary drifters would see it as a good place to spend a couple of nights.'

'The horse tethered at the side of the house belonged to no drifter. It was a fine blue roan. Meant nothing to me then, but a good horse once seen is never forgotten. That same blue roan went through town today.'

'Ridden by a mean man with a moustache,' Paladin said, 'who showed unusual interest in Salty's Notch.'

The widow Bowman-Laing turned to him, looked him up and down with her sharp blue eyes.

'You know,' she said thoughtfully, 'we're going to need a man like you, if you can stay off the drink and find yourself a gun. Because, you mark my words, Paladin: pretty soon now our sleepy world's going to be turned upside down and shaken, and the men responsible won't be taking prisoners.'

TWO

Bushwhack Jack Breaker had chosen a rotting old antebellum mansion as their temporary base. On high ground a mile to the north-east of La Belle Commune, the creaking tumbledown house was shrouded by tall pines planted as windbreaks by the millionaire owner who had died a gallant officer's death in the War Between the States. Squinted at from the coastal strip on which La Belle Commune sprawled, it was lost in those dense trees that were themselves usually a vague shimmer in the constant heat haze, but from the balustraded front balconies supported by fluted Greek columns it was possible to see the distant town.

A town Breaker had steered well clear of on his first visit a couple of weeks ago.

On that occasion the lean, moustachioed outlaw had ridden down from northern Louisiana. Fifteen miles short of La Belle Commune he had made a calculated stop at a small cotton settlement tucked into a lush river valley. He knew nothing about La Belle Commune other than the role it would play in the scheme that would make him rich. What he needed was information. The place to get it was up against the bar in the settlement's only saloon.

It was mid-morning. The grizzled old timer had his foot hooked on a rail. He was willing to talk for as long as his glass was refilled with lukewarm beer. Breaker mentioned La Belle Commune. The old-timer rolled his rheumy eyes and told him that three men long past their best would tell Breaker all he needed to know about La Belle Commune. The town marshal was one; the old-timer couldn't remember his name. Alec Mackie owned the general store, Rik Paulson the saloon.

Without those three men, the old-timer had said, La Belle Commune was a boat without a rudder, a ship without a goddamn sail. And at the old feller's drunken, closing remark, Jack Breaker could barely suppress a grin so close had it come to the image in his mind that was the spur driving him on.

He had slapped the old man on the back, slid a silver dollar along the bar, and once again headed south.

The next evening he had stumbled upon the big house quite by accident as he left the vague trail and cut across country. He had followed a fast flowing creek, watching the foaming water as if hypnotized. His eyes had been drawn to a rickety bridge, little more than a couple of planks without rails; had torn his gaze away and seen the antebellum mansion.

It must once have been pure white. In the gathering gloom it was a drab, peeling grey, its roof and tall chimneys silhouetted against the darkening southern skies. He had ridden away from the bridge and entered the grounds of the old antebellum from the rear, riding across a wide back yard overgrown with weeds, fronting stables with no doors. From the yard he could see past the side of the house and down the slope towards an unseen ocean. He left his horse there, tied to a post, and entered the house through a back door sagging on rusted hinges. He had picked his way past a rear stairway and along a gloomy passageway, climbed a wide staircase that doubled back between floors, on treads that creaked and groaned. He had at once judged that the place was ideal: close to the town, deserted, long forgotten.

On the topmost of the two once elegant front balconies he had stood leaning on the balustrade and smoked a cigar in the cool of evening. As if to prove him wrong, as if to tell him not to count his chickens, some half a mile away down the slope a rider had emerged from a stand of trees. Breaker had stepped back into the shadows, cupping the glow of his cigar. The rider was a woman, wearing a split riding skirt and using a side saddle. She had come close, walking her fine chestnut mare across the rougher ground beyond the edge of the sloping lawns fronting the house. For an instant there was a flash of pale skin and light hair beneath the broad-brimmed hat, and Breaker sensed that she was looking up towards the house. Then she had nudged the big horse to a canter. She had moved quickly down the long slope. Beyond his gaze she seemed to clatter across the shaky bridge without slackening speed and head in a direction that would, Breaker judged, take her back to town.

A town, Breaker had thought at the time, that would nightly be turned a ruddy gold by the setting sun. Which was only fitting. It was gold that had brought him to La

Belle Commune. It was gold that would see him on his way back to Texas a very rich man.

OK. So that had been a couple of weeks ago. Then, he had been a man on a horse feeling his way, looking at possibilities. Now he had with him the men who would help him realize his dream.

The house had enough rooms to house an army, though renegades would be a better way to describe the four men Breaker had enlisted in the New Mexico cantinas and the saloons of southern Texas. Rag tag was a term he had heard bandied among military men. Even that term was paying the lawless band an undeserved compliment.

They had been arriving over the past few days, following the lines on a map Breaker had put before them, then burned. On this, Breaker's second visit to La Belle Commune, he had out of necessity risked riding through the town. For his plan to work and gain him the fortune he had been fighting for all his life, there had to be an easy way down to the shore. That he had spotted the broad trail on his one ride through had made the risk worthwhile. Everything was in place. And one look at the derby-hatted marshal dozing in front of the jail had told him that if the men he had gathered around him formed a rag tag army, then that was all that would be needed to take total control of the town.

Total control was necessary. From what he had seen there would be no resistance. And yet. . . .

In any undertaking, Breaker thought wryly, something unexpected could come leaping out of nowhere to upset the apple-cart. His sight of Paladin in the shadows of the saloon's gallery had been a shock that almost caused a give-away double-take. He's resisted, but that one look had been sufficient. It was Paladin, all right. Looking a bit ragged around the edges, yes, but there was no doubt that his old enemy Paladin was in town.

Yawning, rousing himself with an effort from reverie that was serving no purpose, Breaker said, 'It begins tomorrow. We give the good citizens of La Belle Commune time to wake up. Then we ride in, take over the town, let nobody in or out. All that needs is the removal, permanent' – he looked meaningfully around the watching faces – 'of three ageing has-beens who between 'em run the place.'

'Names?'

'Not needed. The town marshal and two other fellers. One owns the saloon, the other the general store.'

'A kid fresh out of school could do that all on his own with one hand tied – but why would he?' This was a tow-headed gunslinger known only as Deakin. He had skin pitted by smallpox, a voice that set teeth on edge. 'I've been here five days, Breaker. Nothing's moved down there. It's a ghost town, dying in the sun.'

'That's why it was chosen.'

'By you?'

Breaker shook his head. 'No, not by me. But there's something I found out. A drunk in a Las Cruces cantina bartered a fairy story for a drink. I dug deeper, discovered his rambling tale was no made-up story but the honest truth. So I looked at the whys and the wherefores, set those against possibilities and the truly unbelievable outcome.' He grinned. 'That's why we're here.'

It was close to midnight. The five men who had ridden through La Belle Commune one by one were sprawled around a camp-fire built in a stone circle on sloping lawns. Two weeks ago Breaker had looked down on those lawns from the balcony, and a woman on a chestnut mare had crossed them silently and without seeing him. Go back not too many years and those same lawns had been trodden by plantation owners and their ladies. Absurdly rich gentry, they had been waited on by black slaves bearing silver trays loaded with crystal glassware containing the finest imported French wines.

What the four gunslingers were passing from hand to hand, mouth to mouth, was a cracked jug of moonshine whiskey which had been brought in from Texas by a Mexican called Guillermo Rodriguez. He looked little more than a kid, slim in his dark red shirt and tight black pants. His black hair was swept straight back and some kind of perfumed pomade gave it a glossy sheen. A colourful sombrero decorated with silver conchos hung at his back. In the flickering light of the fire Rodriguez was looking at Breaker with undisguised insolence.

'I came at your bidding,' he said, 'but, like Deakin I do not understand how taking over a ghost town can make me a rich man.' In the darkness his white teeth flashed in a broad grin that was a challenge to Breaker. 'If you can explain satisfactorily, it is possible I will decide to remain here.'

'Please yourself,' Breaker said. 'All I'll say is it's not the takeover that'll put gold in your saddle-bags, but what it enables us to do in subsequent days.'

'Subsequent,' another voice echoed, and there was a

ripple of laughter. 'What that means is anyone's guess, so maybe you should let us all into the secret, tell us where this gold's at.'

The man who had spoken was sprawled beyond the reach of the firelight. His black attire left him a vague shape in the shadows. His name was Flint. The light that did reach him glinted on the cold steel of a revolver pouched in leather low on his thigh, on the pallor of his face, on black eyes that were fixed on Breaker.

'What a man doesn't know about,' Breaker said, 'a man can't mess up. A tale told once gets repeated. Passed on. If the wrong person hears it, I've wasted my time.'

'You think one of us would do that?' The firelight flickered in Flint's eyes. There was quiet menace in his voice.

'I'm not prepared to find out. But when the time's right—'

He paused as Lomax, one of the two men closest to the fire, spat his disgust into the flames.

'That's it,' he said, lurching to his feet. 'I'm out of here, look me up next time you're in Galveston—'

Then the breath left his body in an explosive whoosh. A swinging right hook delivered by the other man, a craggy giant called Devlin, took him in the solar plexus and dumped him in the fire. He yowled like a scalded cat, bucked himself out of the embers with the back of his shirt smoking. He rolled in the grass, stopped to glare at the man who had delivered the blow.

Devlin, after taking a careful look at his knuckles, drew deeply on a cigarette and blew a smoke ring at the rising moon. He was still contemplating his artistry when the man he had downed launched himself back across the scattered, glowing embers.

The result was the same. Without disturbing the ash on the cigarette in his left hand, Devlin swayed sideways, delivered a chopping blow to his attacker's neck and watched him drop like a log.

This time he stayed down. One arm had flopped across the fire. Devlin stepped forward to kick it clear, walked a few yards and stood drawing on his cigarette.

'You see,' Flint said softly. 'Lomax wants out, Devlin drops him, but if I'm any judge that big man's of the same opinion. We all are. When the time is right, you say. Let me tell you, Breaker, the right time is now. You wait any longer, there'll be nobody here to listen to your little secret.'

The fire hissed in the silence. A far off coyote howled. From the trees an unseen night bird flapped away into the night. Lomax groaned and rolled over, struggled to rise, made it and stood swaying.

Breaker shook his head, climbed to his feet and stretched.

'If you're right, I'm in trouble, because what's coming can't be handled by a man on his own.' He grinned. 'No, not even by me. Devlin, douse that fire. Then all of you head up to the house. Take the jug to the top balcony, drag out some chairs. You'll see a cigar stub that's been there a couple of weeks. I spent time up there. From that balcony you can see the lights of the town. I'll tell you what's about to happen. Show you as best I can where it's going to take place.'

Breaker hung back. Devlin kicked loose earth over the fire, then followed the others. They went up steps flanked by columns, in through a front door that had once been opened by an English butler.

Those were the days, Breaker thought, following – and for me, something similar is within touching distance. There's a pot of gold waiting at the end of a rainbow. To reach it I've got the help of a mutinous crew, and to make matters worse a man I thought had drowned in the Red River with a couple of bullets in his back is alive and well and living in La Belle Commune. Paladin, who was just about the best bounty hunter in the West.

Now isn't that something to make a man of action lick his lips?

When the talking was over, two men remained on the balcony. Rodriguez was well back against the board walls of the house, sprawled on a chair with worn upholstery through which in places the stuffing had burst. He was smoking a thin black cigarillo. From time to time, his teeth flashed in a grin.

'They are convenient, these balconies,' he said, 'as a way for a man to meet another man's wife with discretion.'

'Never figured you as discreet,' Breaker said.

'If a virile man was in this room, for example, and a beautiful woman in the one below . . .' Rodriguez shrugged eloquently. 'For a strong and agile man to lower himself from this balcony would be the work of a moment.'

'Right now there're no women here,' Breaker said, 'and there's work to be done.'

'Ah yes, and we work well together, you and me,' Rodriguez said softly. 'Me with my reluctance, my apparent desire to be away from here. You with your tales of immense riches.' He chuckled, enjoying what he considered to be a good joke.

At the balcony's ornate balustrade, smoking and staring at an unseen, distant sea, Breaker shook his head impatiently.

'You sure you've got the date right?'

'*Sin duda.* There is no doubt. He drove north from Nicaragua by wagon. A great distance, and always there was the fear of pursuit giving wings to his heels. In Mexico he acquired a caique' – Rodriguez shrugged expansively – 'or maybe not, maybe it was a ketch. *No es importante.* He is sailing from Isla Pajoros, which is an island close to Vera Cruz. His plan is to stay within sight of the coast for most of the way here.'

'Avoiding deep water.'

'*Sí.* He is an excellent sailor, an excellent judge of tides, of prevailing winds. Because of the cargo, he has an arrangement. There will be several men here to meet him.'

'Why La Belle Commune?'

'In Texas, he is a wanted man. Better to be safe. In Louisiana he robbed a bank and as a consequence served time in a Lafayette jail. Later, a free man wandering down the coast, he came across this place. It haunted his imagination, stayed in his mind.'

There was a silence. Breaker flicked his cigarette, watched it spark its way down to the lawns, turned abruptly.

'We've ridden together for a while,' he said, 'but I still don't know what motivates you.'

'It is a family matter.'

'That tells me nothing.'

'A family begins with a father, and a mother.' Rodriguez's white teeth flashed white in the gloom as he drew back his lips in a grimace of hatred. 'At a certain time when I was much younger there were bandits who rode from village to village, killing without discrimination but with much crazy laughter. One hot day it was our pueblo they selected for their amusement. My mother, she was singing quietly to herself as she hung out washing. She was in the way of the bullets they scattered like blind men sowing grain.'

'Mexicans, murdering their own people?' Breaker said. He'd dipped his head. His eyes were hidden, the moustache drooping over lips that had tightened to a thin line.

'But of course not,' Rodriguez said. 'These bandits were *gringos*. Five or six of them, they would come splashing across the Rio Grande with their rebel yells and their bottles of bootleg whiskey. There was one man who was perhaps the worst of the bunch – without him, who knows, maybe there would have been no crazy killing.' He stared hard at Breaker, a thin smile curling his lips. Then he shrugged dismissively as if he had said too much. 'Since then, since the cruel death of our mother, I have grown cold. I care for myself, and the pueblo that is my home, but have a burning hatred of Texans—'

'I was born in Amarillo. That makes me Texan, so why should I trust you?'

'I make exceptions when it is suitable. Without me we would not be here. The trust is in the outcome of our endeavours. We take the town. We wait. A boat arrives. We are rich men.'

'Yeah,' Breaker said. 'A boat carrying a cargo of gold, stolen in Nicaragua, brought north through hostile territories by a thief with cojones. His name is Alvaro Rodriguez. And why I question my trust in you is because that man is your elder brother, and you've sold him down the river.'

THREE

Most days in La Belle Commune begin with the town's sprawl of tumbledown shacks shrouded by a white sea mist. For a while, the air is cool and moist. The temperature drops in bedrooms where sleep has been impossible. Mist curls in through open windows. Skin sticky with night-sweat welcomes the chill. What passes for life in La Belle Commune becomes bearable.

The respite is short lived. The sun pokes its dazzling rim above the eastern horizon and begins its inexorable climb to a zenith. The mist rolls back. Precious moisture evaporates from rusty tin roofs. The packed earth of La Belle Commune's wide thoroughfare begins soaking up the heat that will by mid-morning be strong enough to sear though the thin soles of worn-out boots.

But not Brad Corrigan's. The mist was lingering when he banged open the door and ducked into the small room that was the jail's office. When he pushed back the stiff catch and opened the window he saw that, as on every other morning for as far back as he could remember, the door to Alec Mackie's store was open wide. Directly across the street, Rik Paulson was out on the saloon's gallery smoking his first cigarette of the day. He saw Corrigan, and raised a hand. Corrigan grinned, bowed, and turned away.

The businessmen of La Belle Commune rise early not to serve non-existent customers but to be at their place of work before the heat makes even a short walk a chore.

Without knowing, oblivious to the danger, on this day they had played into the hands of Bushwhack Jack Breaker.

The five men rode down from the trees encircling Emma Bowman-Laing's antebellum mansion as the mist was clearing from the town. They took the raking slopes leading down to the coast at a canter, riding in line abreast when conditions were favourable, at others forming an extended single file. Ahead of them there was no sign of life.

Rodriguez was unconvinced. 'Five men, riding in a bunch, is certain we will be seen,' he said.

'Seeing ain't knowing or understanding,' Breaker said. 'By the time they understand, it'll be too late.'

Acting on Breaker's orders, as they entered the town and clattered past the first shacks in a cloud of dust they broke formation. By the time they'd reached what Breaker thought of with some amusement as the town's business centre, Devlin and Lomax had moved with intent over to the south side of the wide thoroughfare. Deakin was a little way behind them, but in the centre of the road.

Devlin, Lomax and Deakin had been told to keep their guns pouched. On no account were they to resort to gunfire. They were to move as silently as the morning mist.

Flint was with Breaker.

'He was lazing in that rocking chair yesterday, the marshal,' Breaker remarked as he pulled his roan over to the jail and swung down alongside the hitch rail. 'Had his hat tipped, but I saw his eyes watching me. Don't get careless.'

Flint wasn't listening. He'd dismounted swiftly and was in the office ahead of Breaker. When Breaker joined him in an interior where dazzling early morning light created deep shadows in a contrast that confused the eyes, a tall man was coming through an inner doorway. He was wiping shaving suds from his face with a towel. An undershirt hung outside his pants, over narrow hips. Incongruously, considering he had just finished his morning's ablutions, a tired derby hat green with age was perched on his head.

He was, Breaker noted, a good ten feet away from his desk and the coiled belt with its leather holster and pouched six-gun.

'Guess this is where I find out what's going on,' Corrigan said without obvious concern. 'Where're your three outlaw pals?'

'Put your shirt on, Marshal,' Flint said softly. 'We're going for a ride in the country.'

'Need to walk a bit first,' Corrigan said, his pale blue eyes straying towards the desk. 'I've an arrangement with a feller called Shorty Long. Got something passes for a barn behind his ruin of a house. He acts as the town hostler. Folk pay him a dollar now and then to look after their horses.' He was watching Breaker. 'Shorty spends a lot of time over at the saloon. Takes some effort to rouse him before noon.'

He had been talking easily, scrubbing his chin with the towel, moving towards the desk.

'Where?'

Corrigan grinned at Breaker. 'Thataway,' he said, jerking his thumb towards the east side of town. 'Fifty yards down the road. If your ride in the country is going to take us to the Widow Bowman-Laing's old house,' he said knowingly, 'Shorty's place is on the way.'

Hand still raised, still talking, he stepped sideways with deceptive speed and threw the towel across Breaker's face. A continuation of the movement turned into a lunge for his desk and the six-gun. His hand slapped the leather holster. Breaker was cursing, fumbling with the damp cloth. Flint, a thin smile on his face, went for his six-gun. His hand was a blur, but Corrigan caught the anticipated move. His long leg lashed out. The toe of his boot caught Flint's wrist as his fingers touched the gun's butt. The outlaw pulled his hand away and swore through clenched teeth.

Corrigan swept his six-gun off the desk. It was still inside its holster. That didn't deter the tall marshal. With the heavy gun-belt loaded with shells flapping loose he thumbed the six-gun's hammer. His first shot tore through the leather, clipped Breaker's shoulder and shattered the half-open window. Broken glass caught the sunlight as it tinkled into the street. Breaker, face twisted with pain, stumbled backwards into a chair and fell flat on his back.

Flint, right hand deadened by Corrigan's kick, reached awkwardly across with his left hand and dragged out his

Colt. It jerked free of leather, but was upside down in his hand. Now it was Corrigan's turn to grin. With one eye on Breaker he unhurriedly turned his six-gun on the black-clad outlaw. That supreme confidence was his undoing. Flint didn't waste time bringing his Colt into a firing position. He took one step towards Corrigan and whipped his left arm around in a vicious backhand blow. The Colt connected with Corrigan's cheekbone with a terrible crack of metal on bone. The marshal's eyes glazed. Blood streamed from the gash opened by the Colt's sharp front sight. He lost his grip on the six-gun and wobbled on legs drained of strength.

A murderous gleam in his eyes, Flint used the recoil from his first blow to deliver a second that opened a bloody gash on the other side of Corrigan's face. It drove Corrigan backwards and sideways. Already falling, he hit the side of his desk and lay in a crumpled heap on the office's dirt floor.

'He's done,' Breaker growled. He was up off the floor, his hand feeling his shoulder and coming away slick with blood. 'Get outside. You and Deakin find that hostler's place, tip the old man out of his cot, get him to bring out three horses.'

Flint shook his head. 'You go tell him. I'm not your messenger boy.'

'Jesus Christ,' Breaker said. 'OK, so poke your head out the door and call Deakin over.'

'This once,' Flint said, heading for the door. 'I'm here to get rich, not take orders.'

'Yeah, well, while we're establishing rules, next time go easy on the gun-whipping. You hit this feller too hard. We

31

need him on his feet for a while longer. If there's water in a bowl out back I'll give him his second wash of the day. He won't know it, but it'll be the last of his miserable life.'

Across the street, the giant Devlin had tied his horse then climbed a few creaking steps and entered into the cool of the general store. He was greeted by the usual store smells of raw kerosene, lye soap, grain stored in sacks, the leather of shiny new waist-belts and boots. A burly man with a florid face was behind the counter. Wire-framed glasses were perched on the end of his nose. He was attending to paperwork.

He looked up at Devlin's approach, straightened, smiled a polite welcome with his eyebrows raised in an unspoken query. Devlin wasn't fooled. With instinct honed by years on the owlhoot trail he'd detected the sudden wariness in the storekeeper's manner.

'Mornin' sir,' Devlin said. 'What I want is the makings. Couple of sacks of Bull Durham, papers to go with the baccy.' He dropped a hand to his pocket, jingled coins.

'That's the way,' the storekeeper said. 'Me, I can't stand a feller who chews then spits, filthy habit, rots teeth, the Lord only knows what it does to a man's insides. . . .'

While talking he'd taken half a step backwards and was now bending to reach under the counter. Devlin was highly amused. The tobacco he'd asked for was displayed on shelves against the back wall, so what the hell was this feller doing down there? Devlin, knowing the answer to that question, stepped closer to the counter. The burly man straightened. His eyes had narrowed. The muscles in his jaw were bunched. He brought up both hands, fast. He was holding an ancient sawn-off shotgun.

'Hell fire,' Devlin said, 'that's no way to treat a cus-tomer,' and without pause or effort he launched a looping punch with his massive right fist. It cracked solidly against Mackie's jaw. His eyes rolled back in his head. The shotgun clattered to the counter, slid to the floor. Mackie stumbled backwards, crashed against the shelves of tobacco and went down in a shower of Bull Durham sacks.

Shaking his head, Devlin went around the counter. Mackie was out cold, face down. Devlin took hold of the storekeeper's collar, dragged him the length of the store's rough dirt floor and dumped him outside on the narrow gallery.

Then he straightened, flexed his muscles, and looked expectantly across at the jail.

The lingering smell of cigarette smoke on the saloon's gallery warned Rodriguez that someone was up and about. Ignoring Breaker's warning, he loosened his six-gun. Then he pushed through the half-closed door into an inte-rior that was dark enough to convince a man he'd gone blind. But that was the contrast between the dazzling outside sunlight and the deep shadows in a room without windows. It took but a few seconds for Rodriguez's eyes to adjust.

A man was leaning against the bar, watching him. He was tall, gaunt. A smouldering cigarette drooped from his lips. He slapped a wet cloth noisily down on the crude wooden bar, picked up a shiny pick helve and walked towards Rodriguez.

'I know you,' he said.

Rodriguez raised an eyebrow. 'That is most strange. I have not seen you before in my life, and I am a man who remembers most things very easily.'

'Correction,' the tall man said. 'I don't know you, but I saw you ride through town a couple of days ago. Figured you for an outlaw. Wondered where you were heading.'

Rodriguez grinned. 'Then this is your lucky day, *mi amigo*. You are about to find out.'

'You telling, or showing?'

'With words, I am not too good.'

'That's not the impression I get.' The saloonist stepped closer, waggled the helve. 'And I'm choosy about where I go, and who I go with.'

'But also I think you are curious.' Rodriguez saw the instant narrowing of the man's eyes. 'You wish to know what is about to happen to your tired, dirty town. If you are genuinely curious, then going with me will provide the answer.'

'There's a man upstairs who'd like to be in on this. You look hot. Buy yourself a drink, I'll go fetch him—'

He broke off. With uncanny speed Rodriguez had drawn his six-gun and rammed it up under the tall man's chin. He thrust with strength, forcing Paulson's head back. With great deliberation, watching Paulson's eyes, he cocked the weapon.

'Let your useless piece of wood fall to the floor,' Rodriguez said. 'Then, without being foolish, without for example making any noise that might alert that man you mentioned, walk towards the door. I will be behind you. If you make one wrong move, I will blow a big hole in the back of your head out of which your brains will leak. But that will not concern you, for you will indeed be very dead.'

The five men rode out of town retracing their earlier route, but now they were eight. The hostler called Shorty had directed Deakin to the horses belonging to the marshal, Mackie and Paulson. Then he had spat wetly in the dust of his barn and told the outlaw if he wanted them saddled he could damn well go right ahead and do it himself.

Deakin was dripping with sweat when he led the three horses down the street to the jail. Bushwhack Jack Breaker had been waiting impatiently. Now he brought out the marshal, who had shakily donned his shirt. Already it was soaked with blood. Rodriguez came across the street from the saloon, Paulson walking nonchalantly ahead of him with the cigarette still drooping from his thin lips. From the general store, Devlin led a dazed storekeeper who stumbled as he walked and had blood trickling from the corner of his mouth.

Flint noted that with interest.

'Guess I'm not the only one who hits hard. Maybe there's a lesson for you there, Breaker.'

'Shut up. Get these men mounted, and let's get out of here.'

And so, within minutes, the three men Breaker considered were those he needed out of the way were in the saddle and the eight men jogged down the centre of the wide street and on out of town. And again it was the loquacious Rodriguez who opened his mouth to comment.

'Hey, Breaker,' he said, 'maybe you were right after all.

In and out, an hour total – and the only ones saw us are these three fellers here.'

'You believe that,' Breaker said, 'then you're not only the youngest Mex I ever hitched up with, you're not only the most treacherous, double-crossing back-stabbing Mex I ever met, you're also the dumbest – and believe me, kid, that's saying something.'

FOUR

Paladin was scratching his head and yawning as he clumped down the saloon's steep, narrow back stairs. They led into the kitchen, and halfway down he was already sniffing for the smell of frying ham and eggs, listening for the mouth-watering sizzle but hearing nothing.

Rik Paulson knew what time Paladin rolled out of bed – could probably set his battered turnip watch by that regularity – and when Paladin came down he would be preparing breakfast for both of them with ash from his dangling cigarette threatening to fall into the frying pan of hot food and speckle egg yolks with grey.

Not today. Paladin took in the kitchen's emptiness, then walked through frowning. He absently brushed a handle and set the empty black pan spinning and wobbling as he passed the stove, listened to the ringing clatter of metal on metal, pushed through into the saloon's bar, and stopped.

The smell of cigarette smoke. Not stale, not the smell of the cigar stub Shorty Long invariably crushed under his boot before walking out at midnight with his limping gait exaggerated by drink. So it was smoke from Paulson's cigarette. The saloon-keeper was up – but where the hell was he?

There was a wet cloth on the bar. Cleaning the drink-ringed surface was a morning chore – but it was unfinished, perhaps not even started, because some of last night's glasses were still standing empty and stained. Puzzled, Paladin went on through and out on to the gallery, wincing as the heat of the sun hit him and almost took his breath away.

Across the street, an empty rocking chair. Well, that signified nothing. It was afternoon when Brad Corrigan sat outside rocking and snoozing. But he was a stickler for closing doors. This morning the jail's door, Paladin noted, was wide open – and that was unheard of. However, he mused, for five Texan outlaws to ride through La Belle Commune on successive days was also unprecedented.

As Paladin walked thoughtfully down the steps and set off across the street he had the disturbing conviction that the coming of five outlaws, and an unexpectedly open door, were in some way connected.

Inside the jail office Paladin got the eerie feeling that he was in a room empty because of tragedy – and with a shattered window he noted somewhat belatedly. Foreboding piling on foreboding he thought, moving slowly about the room, skirting the desk, poking his head and shoulders briefly through the inner door leading to the building's only cell and seeing nothing to raise hackles.

But back in the room and this time using his eyes he saw clear evidence of violence.

The desk had been pushed out of position. It was a heavy, solid oak piece of furniture. Something had banged against it with considerable force, sliding it across the dirt floor; the movement was marked by grooves. Then, in the space between the desk's front and the open window, the floor was stained with spots of blood. A crumpled white towel lay close to the stains. When Paladin picked it up he could feel the damp, smell the soap the marshal always used for his morning's ablutions.

The front door banged against the wall.

Paladin swung around, his right hand slapping his hip. But there was no holster there, no six-gun. His hand brushed only the worn cloth of his pants, and a rueful smile twisted his lips as his heart hammered.

'Didn't hear you come in, Emma.'

'I know. And don't for goodness sake give that to me,' she said, her eyes on the towel. 'The last thing I want is for you to see me shed tears.'

Paladin dropped the damp cloth on a chair.

'Why would you shed tears? Do you know something about what's happened here?'

Emma Bowman-Laing moved into the room gliding silently on worn sandals hidden by her long cotton frock. Her hands were restless. First she fiddled with a wisp of grey hair that had escaped the tortoiseshell combs she wore that morning. Then, as if aware that she was revealing her agitation, she flattened her palms on the thin cloth covering her thighs.

She shook her head. 'I know nothing about what happened in here, but I saw five men ride into town. When they rode out again, not thirty minutes later, they were eight.'

'Ah.' Paladin nodded slowly. 'Five plus three: Corrigan, Mackie, Paulson.'

'Taken, against their will.' Her stare was scathing. 'Alec Mackie was there, looking dazed. Brad didn't look . . . didn't look himself. And his face was bloodied.' There was a catch in her voice. She struggled for composure. 'And Rik Paulson, I saw him, and he was looking very angry indeed.'

'I can understand that,' Paladin said. 'He didn't get around to frying his breakfast or mine, and a hungry man—'

'Oh for God's sake!'

'I'm making light of a situation that we know nothing about,' Paladin said. 'Giving way to panic won't help—'

'How dare you! It seemed to me when I saw those riders that there was only one man left in town I could turn to. If you define that as panic then maybe I should have looked elsewhere. Tell me, Paladin, do you think I might be better off talking to Shorty Long? He's a cantankerous, gimpy sonofabitch, but by God he's got guts.'

Paladin's lips were twitching. Emma Bowman-Laing, using strong language? Another first, on a day rich in precedents.

He sighed, dragged a hand across his face.

'I apologize. My old friends, the men who make this town, have been by taken by hard men who used violence. You say Brad's face was bloodied, and it's clear that blood was spilled here, in this office.'

'They crossed the bridge over Petit Creek,' Bowman-Laing said. 'You know what I saw on my evening ride a couple of weeks ago: a man, that man with the blue roan,

40

on the balcony of my old house. Drawing the obvious con-
clusion, that's where Brad and the others have been taken.
There, or the hunting lodge in the woods, perhaps . . .'
She trailed off, frowning.

'But why? Not why there, but why anywhere? What the
hell is going on in La Belle Commune?'

'Go and find out,' Bowman-Laing said bluntly.

'There are five of them, all outlaws. If I go, I need the
cover of darkness.'

'For those friends of yours, that could be too late.'

'If I'm the only man you could turn to, I'll be little use
dead.'

Bowman-Laing pursed her lips, moved restlessly. She
picked up the damp towel, pressed it to her lips, then
folded it neatly and placed it on the corner of the desk.

'I heard a name.'

'What?'

'Those ruffians, those outlaws, they were talking when
they rode past my house. There's a young Mexican, greasy
hair and a fancy sombrero.' She looked hard at Paladin.
'He was in high spirits, called across to that lean man with
the black hat and the moustache – the one on the blue
roan who was last to arrive, do you remember him?'

'I didn't see him all that clearly,' Paladin said, wondering where this was leading.

'No,' Bowman-Laing said acidly, 'I shouldn't expect too
much, should I?'

'Go on,' Paladin said impatiently.

'The young Mexican spoke quite clearly. The moustachioed outlaw's name is Breaker.' She raised an eyebrow,
looked knowingly at Paladin. 'Tell me, does that mean

anything to a man who, Brad once told me, hunted wanted killers for bounty all across Texas?'

Paladin felt his stomach tighten, the muscles across his back clench. His mouth dry, he said, 'A man called Breaker shot me in the back, then tried to finish me off by drowning. He, or one of his men, tossed me into the Red.'

'And Petit Creek runs close to the house,' Bowman-Laing said. 'On my nightly rides I cross the bridge on the trail out of town, take some thoughtful time on what used to be my property and come back by way of the old bridge put across the creek by my granddaddy.'

'Very old,' Paladin said, 'and very shaky. One of these days that bridge will give and dump you in the creek.'

'The water there, like the Red,' she said, her eyes bleak, 'is quite deep.'

Paladin nodded. 'Yesterday you said that men like those who rode through town don't take prisoners. That was your judgement, and it's close to the truth. If this is the same Breaker and he's the *honcho* like me and Brad figured, unless someone gets to them mighty fast our three friends are as good as dead.'

FIVE

'The problem I am aware of,' young Rodriguez said, 'is that by removing those men from town we have taken prisoners who must be guarded constantly. However, as it is the town of La Belle Commune we were supposed to be guarding, I see that there is considerable disruption to your plans. Lock-down is impossible in the situation you have created.'

'Bullshit,' Breaker said.

'You're talking through your backside, Kid,' Flint said. 'I can tell you now the problem you're aware of will be short-lived.'

At that a light sparked in Breaker's dark eyes, and he nodded. 'Nightfall puts an end to it, over and done with.'

They were again gathered on the lawn in front of the antebellum mansion. But tonight it was just Breaker, Flint and the kid sitting smoking around the camp-fire. Devlin, Lomax and Deakin were inside the house, playing cards outside the locked door of a windowless back room that had once been a larder.

Rodriguez had spread his hands in an eloquent gesture

of confusion.

'All right,' Breaker said, 'we could have plugged all three of 'em in town. But I asked for them to be taken quietly because three men gunned down in their place of work would've brought people tumbling out of their beds. I didn't want that, wouldn't have done us any good. That shot fired by Corrigan was inside, muffled, went unheard. We were in and out, nobody the wiser.'

'I'm beginning to doubt your judgement,' Flint said. 'Rodriguez made the point when we were riding in: somebody must have seen us. And people are going to ask questions when three old citizens disappear and we put a guard both ends of town.'

'If they do, we say it's for their own good. We tell 'em a band of renegades is heading for La Belle Commune. We're there to keep them out.'

'And the three men we have taken?' Flint said. 'What was that for?'

'Town leaders. Removed to a place of safety, because when those renegades ride in they'd be obvious targets and in danger.'

Rodriguez was grinning. 'And now it is my turn to say bullshit. If I was talking through my backside, you are most assuredly talking through your hat.'

'Yeah, well, enough of that,' Breaker snapped.

He flicked his cigarette end into the fire and climbed to his feet, looked across at the Mexican.

'Get up to the house, tell the others to bring 'em out. Stick around, but back off so if there's trouble you can see it coming and act. Flint, I want you at the bottom of those steps.'

Rodriguez jogged away, up between the fluted columns and into the house. Flint moved lazily but with his six-gun already out and held against his thigh. Breaker turned away. In the gathering darkness he looked west across the lawns. He could hear the waters of Petit Creek, knew exactly where the rickety bridge crossed the deeper water, but could see no details in the fading light. He took a deep breath, paced restlessly, pulling absently at his moustache and thinking of Rodriguez and the questions he had asked.

Breaker smiled thinly in the gloom.

He wanted the three townsmen dead. That would wipe out the admittedly unlikely possibility of anyone whipping up an armed force to oppose the outlaws. Well, almost, Breaker thought grimly. Paladin would be rooming somewhere close to where he bought his drinks. A bounty hunter, no matter how long ago he'd hung up his guns, would be snapped from sleep by gunfire. He would come tumbling out of his bed, hit the street pulling up his pants and holding a cocked six-gun. And Paladin was a fighter. Up against five men, he would have gone down in a hail of lead – but he would have taken two, maybe three of Breaker's men with him.

As for the band of renegades about to threaten the town, well, there was some truth in that. The boat carrying the elder Rodriguez brother would be met. He would have made certain that the men employed to transport his stolen gold across country would be armed and dangerous.

Breaker was feeling halfway satisfied with the way things were going when a sudden crash from inside the house snapped his head around. Flint had tensed and was looking up at the door. Breaker stayed were he was, but he was watching and listening and his hand had moved to his six-gun.

'They're coming.'

Brad Corrigan was whispering into almost total darkness. It was like conversing at the bottom of a deep well. To one side there was a sliver of light showing beneath the locked door. A shadow had moved across it. Now Brad and his fellow prisoners heard the jingle of keys.

'Won't be the five of them,' Rik Paulson said. 'Two, three at most, and there's three of us.'

'Unarmed,' Mackie pointed out.

'But desperate.' Corrigan said bleakly. 'Don't know about you, but that gives me the strength of ten men.'

'You've got your mind on the Widder Bowman-Laing,' Paulson said.

'Yeah, and the image of that elegant old gal heats my blood more than a few sacks of coarse flour or a bottle of bootleg whiskey.'

'Each to his own,' Paulson said, smacking his lips noisily, but Brad knew the talk and the joshing was merely a futile effort to settle jangling nerves.

'Just to make it clear,' Corrigan said in his town-marshal voice, 'don't anyone do anything foolish, one wrong—'

Then the door was flung open with a crash. Dazzled by lamplight that at other times would have had them cursing and winding up the wick, they made no move. Then Paulson swore, leaped past Corrigan and charged.

There were three men in the passageway, two of then

holding six-guns. Paulson's rush took the two in front by surprise. He hit the smaller man like a charging longhorn steer. His shoulder rammed into the man's midriff, driving the breath explosively from his body. At the same time his right arm came around in a raking punch that threatened to remove the man's head.

It didn't connect. A craggy giant of a man had watched with amusement as his companion doubled up, gasping. Then he casually swiped Paulson across the back of the neck with the barrel of his six-gun. Paulson went down, his body flopping limply. The outlaw grinned, cocked his pistol and turned it on Corrigan and Mackie.

'Anyone else gonna try?'

Mackie was raging. Ignoring the gun pointing at his head, the storekeeper tried to force his way past Corrigan.

'Out of the damn way,' he snarled, using his elbow on the marshal, knocking him back against the door jamb.

Corrigan braced himself, then stopped Mackie cold with a stiff arm across the throat.

'Shut up,' he snapped, 'and use your goddamn eyes.'

A tow-headed outlaw, his countenance ruined by small-pox, was watching from a little way back, his eyes revealing a hungry lust to kill. At the far end of the passageway, in the faint light near the front door, a young Mexican was grinning happily, teeth white in the gloom. He wore tight black pants, a loose red shirt, and he, too, exuded an air of menace. His six-gun was shiny, with a white ivory butt. He was spinning it on his forefinger. In the opinion of Brad Corrigan, that young man was another who would take great joy in killing.

The outlaw who had taken the blow in the solar plexus

had recovered and, glaring balefully down on Paulson, now drew his own weapon. The saloon keeper was groaning and struggling to get his knees under him. The big outlaw leaned down, grabbed him by his shirt collar and effortlessly hauled him to his feet. Paulson sagged back against the wall. He was massaging the back of his neck and trying to shake the cobwebs out of his head.

'They are most amusing games you play,' the young Mexican called, 'but I am of the opinion that Breaker will by now be impatient. Is possible we move now?'

'You heard him,' the big man said, and he waggled his six-gun. 'It's time for an evening stroll by the creek,' he added, and behind him the man with the pockmarked face chuckled. It was like a coughing, rasping wheeze. It chilled Brad Corrigan to the bone.

Petit Creek. As he, Mackie and Paulson allowed themselves to be herded out of the room and into the cool fresh air of a Louisiana summer's night, Corrigan traced the creek's course in his mind. He recalled how it tumbled down the slope to the west and north of the big antebellum mansion, was crossed by a crude plank bridge, then flowed onwards and downwards to cross the trail out of La Belle Commune and enter the sea to the east of Salty's Notch.

The creek lay on what had been Emma Bowman-Laing's land. She had first become aware of it as a small child with pigtails and skinny legs and a bright smile, and it was now an essential part of her regular evening rides. But talk of an evening stroll spoken by a muscular giant of an outlaw with a six-gun in his big fist carried with it hidden menace; menace Brad Corrigan could sense but,

48

like everything that had happened since he had been taken from the familiarity of his jail's office, did not understand.

They clattered down the steps to be met by the rawboned outlaw with the moustache and flat-crowned hat and unmistakable air of authority. The *honcho*, Corrigan thought; Breaker, the young Mex had called him. This man Breaker said nothing. The three men were ushered across the lawn. A rising moon softened by thin cloud cast faint shadows. Paulson stumbled, still weak from the cruel blow. Behind them the big outlaw chuckled. Someone was whistling through his teeth. Tuneless. Irritating.

Realization of what was happening to them hit Brad Corrigan with a suddenness that threatened to take the strength from his long legs. He thought about Emma Bowman-Laing and what might have been, and he was overwhelmed by sadness. By the light of the rising moon they were being herded like sheep across lawns and rough pasture. By a creek with a romantic name out of Louisiana's French past, they would be shot. Their bodies would be dumped in the cold waters and, as far as Corrigan could tell, there wasn't a damn thing they could do to save themselves.

Paladin and Shorty Long heard the first shot as the moon floated clear of thin cloud and lit the broken roof of Bowman-Laing's old house. They had circled around, first taking the trail east and crossing the town bridge over Petit Creek. Then they had reined their horses around in a northerly direction and, in darkness, worked their way up the gentle grassy slopes towards the Bowman-Laing land.

The sound that reached their ears to cast a cold chill over the night and set already tense nerves tingling was the sharp crack of a handgun. As to direction, Paladin estimated that it came from somewhere close to Grandaddy Bowman-Laing's bridge that crossed Petit Creek under a thick tangle of tall trees. Had to be there, Paladin thought bitterly, because Bushwhack Jack Breaker was nothing if not consistent in his methods.

He flashed a quick glance at Shorty Long. The hostler nodded.

'Just the one,' he said. 'One shot on its own don't make a gunfight, and that's worrying. In the circumstance I'd say it signifies a killing.'

'If it does,' Paladin said, 'very soon there'll be two more.'

Emma had left Corrigan's jail in considerable agitation after Paladin had made his gloomy prophecy. Moments later Paladin had taken a rifle from Brad Corrigan's gun rack, a couple of boxes of shells from a cupboard, and crossed the street to his room over the empty saloon. There he slid open the drawer beneath the washstand and took out the worn gun-belt with its loops filled with brass shells, and the Colt .45 that had lain there, wrapped in oily rags, for the better part of two years.

He had strapped on the gun-belt and tied the holster's thongs around his thigh; adjusted the way the revolver hung so that the butt could be brushed by a relaxed right hand; felt satisfied, but awkward after so long away from any weapon. Then, armed but with no clear idea of what to do, he had again clattered down the stairs and out into the baking heat of the shaded gallery.

He had been met by Shorty Long.

The hostler was a wiry man with bow legs and crinkly grey hair. Somewhere in his forties, he had sharp blue eyes and a gammy right leg. Like many wranglers, he had been left crippled by years spent breaking wild broncs, and had turned naturally to his present occupation as a safe way of working with the horses that were his life.

Long had a six-gun tucked in the waistband of his pants, and was carrying an old Henry rifle. Emma Bowman-Laing, he said, had stopped by his stables on the way to her town house, quickly apprised him of the situation, and he'd come a-running.

They'd spent the rest of the day kicking their heels, Paladin knowing instinctively that Bushwhack Jack Breaker would make no move before nightfall. He was optimistic, because at the worst of times he looked for a bright side, and the arrival of Long had boosted his hopes. Three men had been taken, all of them old-timers. Breaker was an outlaw without soul, but would he kill three men in cold blood? Paladin couldn't see that happening. His assessment of the situation was that Breaker had taken the men to keep them away from town – for reasons unknown. If Paladin was right, locking them in the big house would do that, without bloodshed.

Now, as the crack of the gunshot fired somewhere close to Petit Creek faded from ears but remained to haunt the memory, the little hostler showed his mettle.

'Two more shots will mean three men dead,' he growled. 'I ain't got enough friends to let that happen.'

Despite his gammy leg he rode as if born in the saddle. He used his spurs and was away up the slope before

51

Paladin could react. Paladin, after a moment's hesitation, set off after the little man.

No more shots had been fired. But the night was almost too quiet and that, Paladin knew, meant there was a need for caution in their approach.

'Ease back, Shorty,' Paladin said, overtaking Long and cutting across towards the gurgling and rushing of the unseen creek. 'The trees here will serve us well. The creek's pretty well flanked by 'em on both sides, all along its course until it reaches town. We should be able to get close without being seen – but not on horseback.'

'I'm not a walking man, Paladin, and for the sake of those poor fellers out there what we need most of all is speed.'

But Paladin was already out of the saddle and slipping his rifle from its boot. The horse moved away at a walk, head high, reins trailing. Paladin jogged silently over to the first line of trees and into the shadows. Twigs snapped underfoot, and he cursed softly. He could smell dead, fallen leaves, the waters of the creek. He waited there, looking up the slope with straining eyes as Shorty Long dismounted and slapped his horse's rump. When he came towards the trees he was carrying the old Henry rifle and limping badly.

'We're closer than I thought,' Paladin said softly, resting a hand on Long's shoulder. 'There's a break in the trees' – he pointed – 'and I thought I saw movement. Higher up, on this side of the creek but up above where the bridge crosses.'

Even as he spoke the night was split by the crack of a second shot. They were now much closer to the gunman.

The detonation was again from a handgun, but shocking in its intensity. In the fraction of a second before the sound reached their ears their eyes narrowed as a muzzle flash lit up the night. The dazzling light gave them the exact location of the men they were hunting. It took a second or so for their eyes to readjust. Then, cautiously, they edged closer to the break in the trees. The sight that met their eyes hit them hard, took away their breath.

'Jesus bloody H Christ,' Shorty Long whispered.

The moon had climbed higher so that its wan light now shone down on a natural clearing in the woods. The shadows of the high branches of trees forming a semi-circle around the clearing painted skeletal patterns of light and shade on the grass. The clearing was the site the long-dead Bowman-Laing had chosen for his bridge over the creek.

Bushwhack Jack Breaker had chosen it as a place of execution.

Two men were struggling under the dead weight of a man's body. Hats pushed back from foreheads glistening with sweat they were making for the trees higher up the slope, stumbling and cursing. There a big man waited, hands on hips.

In the centre of the clearing, a young Mexican with the build of a dancer had a shiny pistol thrust up under Brad Corrigan's rib cage. His greased black hair was glossy in the moonlight. He was grinning, his eyes on the two men and their burden.

Breaker was a few yards away from the Mexican and Corrigan. The flat-crowned black hat was firm on his head and placed his face in shadow out of which his eyes glittered. A cigar jutted from under his drooping moustache, the end glowing as he breathed. In the weak light he was as lean as a peeled pole. His six-gun was pouched. He stood with folded arms.

Brad Corrigan's tarnished badge of office was pinned to Breaker's vest.

'Dammit, we gotta do something, Paladin,' Long mumbled, dropping to one knee, fumbling with the Henry repeater. 'That feller there's the one doin' the shootin', the killing—'

'Wait.' Paladin grabbed his arm, felt the little man's muscles taut with tension, held him still with an effort. 'The man they're carrying into the trees is dead. I think it's Mackie. If it is, the first shot we heard did for Paulson. They're both finished, there's nothing we can do to help those two—'

'So we move damn fast to help Brad, and now's the time—'

'No.'

'Yes, for Christ's sake, two of 'em have their hands full carrying Mac, the Mex' is holdin' Brad and that other bastard of a killer is too busy watchin' the fun.'

'And if we open up we have to make damn sure one of us kills that Mexican kid with the first shot, or he just pulls the trigger and blows Brad's head off his shoulders.' Paladin tightened his grip. 'We wait, Shorty. When it's time for Breaker—'

'Who?'

'Bushwhack Jack Breaker. A killer who thought he'd done for me. I'm here out of his past as living proof he can be beaten. What I'm saying is when it's time for Breaker to plug Brad, that Mex' has to get out of the way, stand well clear. When he does. . . .'

'Yeah,' Long breathed, reluctantly nodding agreement, seeing the sense in what Paladin was saying. He relaxed a little. Rested the Henry with its butt on the grass. Then he leaned on the rifle. But he hadn't planted it firmly, and the grass was already damp with dew. The butt slid under the hostler's weight. He fell sideways. Knowing the need for silence, he kept his mouth clamped shut. But he was close to the trees. He fell heavily into dry undergrowth. The noise was like the fierce crackling of a raging scrub fire.

The Mex's head shot around.

'Somebody is there watching, Breaker,' he called and, stepping away from Brad Corrigan, he snapped his pistol down and began shooting. As fast as he acted, he was still no match for Breaker. Before the warning shout had faded Breaker was turning and crouching, firing at the break in the trees, fanning the hammer of his six-gun with the heel of his hand so that shots came fast and furious.

The two men who had been carrying Paulson's body were running out of the trees, drawing their guns. They were followed by the big man.

'All five of them,' Paladin cursed.

He took a step backwards out of the light of the moon and began shooting. Shorty Long was still down and swearing furiously, but he had rolled on to his belly and was triggering the big old Henry.

It was a game the outlaws were used to playing. Accustomed to dealing with armed posses intent on stringing them up, they were unfazed by gunfire from a ring-rusty bounty hunter and a crippled wrangler. They scattered. Each man made good use of deceptive shadows, all the while moving without haste towards them.

Paladin and Long were not hitting their targets. Outnumbered and out-gunned, they were firing while slowly retreating through the trees lining the creek. For Long, that was difficult. The Henry was an awkward weapon to fire when standing up, much more so for a lame man walking backwards. The outlaws could not see them, but the hail of lead they were pouring into the timber was deadly. Under snapped orders from Breaker they had spit into groups of two. Beginning on the left and right flanks, each pair was firing spaced shots, working their way inwards. It was a clever move.

But men crossing open ground under fire, however wild, are bound to suffer casualties. Paladin grunted in satisfaction as he took careful aim and one of the outlaws threw up his hands and went down in a heap. His well-placed shot had an immediate effect. Outlaws following Breaker's orders and advancing in an orderly fashion scattered like leaves in the wind. They sought cover. Paladin sent them on their way with a volley of shots that emptied his gun.

'Go for the horses, Shorty,' he said, shouting above the crackle of gunfire, ducking as an incoming bullet sent white splinters flying. 'I'll keep plugging away, hold these fellers off as long as I can. When you've brought those horses close, give a whistle and I'll come running.'

He watched the little hostler grin and slip away through the trees carrying the useless rifle. When he turned back to face the clearing Paladin realized the situation had changed. The gunfire had become spasmodic. Then it ceased altogether. In the sudden deadening silence his ringing ears caught the sound of excited voices. Moving through acrid, drifting gunsmoke, he edged back to the opening in the trees, reloading from his gun-belt.

At once he was hit by a surge of hope.

Brad Corrigan had made a break for freedom. Taking advantage of the diversion created by Paladin and Long, he must have first backed slowly away from the Mexican kid until there was plenty of space between them. Now he was running. Clutching the incongruous derby hat in one hand, Corrigan was making for the bridge. He hurdled the body of the outlaw Paladin had downed and kept on running. Though a man slowed by age, his long, raking strides were eating up the ground.

It was again the alert Mexican kid who had first spotted Corrigan's move. It was the Mexican who cut short the escape. Moving as if he had all the time in the world, he coolly took aim and fired two shots. Paladin was helpless, caught in the act of reloading. Unable to do anything to save the man, he watched the bullets hit Corrigan as he neared the bridge. The marshal arched his back at the terrible impact, continued running but the strength had leaked from his bony frame. He fought to keep going, but it was momentum driving him and his long legs were buckling. Then his feet became tangled in the coarse wet grass. He pitched head first over the bank alongside the bridge, catching the timber with his shoulder and twisting as he fell. There was a splash. A gout of water glistened in the strengthening moonlight.

His old hat, dropped from a nerveless hand, wobbled its way across the grass and came to rest against the single wooden step that led on to the bridge.

A thin whistle from close by dragged Paladin away as the other outlaws came out from cover and gathered around Breaker and the kid. Pouching the six-gun, he threaded his way through the trees and out on to the open grass where Long was waiting with the horses.

The little hostler was up in the saddle where he was at home, looking questioningly at Paladin. Paladin shook his head. He took the reins from Long, thrust a foot into a stirrup and quickly mounted. His mind was numb. He couldn't look the other man in the face. Not fifteen minutes ago he had told the hostler that he, Paladin, was living proof that Bushwhack Jack Breaker could be beaten. Yet, when put to the test, he could only watch a cold-blooded killing while fumbling with brass shells and an empty gun.

Hell, he had been no more than thirty yards from the Mex and he was incapable of firing a single shot to save the man who was his best friend.

'Back to town?' Long said.

Paladin took a breath. He glanced back across wet grass to the trees, visualizing the clearing that lay beyond them and had been the scene of brutal killings. As if to taunt him, the stink of cordite lingered in his nostrils; his ears rang to the echoes of gunfire. Above that ringing he heard the rise and fall of distant voices, but not the crackle of timber that would signify pursuit.

He turned in the saddle to look the other way, towards the moonlit antebellum, thought about the imponder-ables and the questions that remained unanswered. About the town of La Belle Commune, and where it fitted into

Bushwhack Jack Breaker's plans – and admitted to being stumped.

He shook his head. 'No,' he said, thinking hard. 'I can see it now. They've got rid of Corrigan, Paulson and Mackie to make it easier for them to take the town – though God knows why they'd want to do that. But it's the town they want, and that's where they'll go.'

'But first they'll come after us.'

'Maybe – maybe not.'

Long swore. 'OK. But if they were using the antebellum their horses are up there, by the old stables. They're forced to go to the house, so I say we get away from here, and fast.'

'We could do that, but there's more to it than saving our hides. It's a question of where we're better off, now, and in the days to come. Breaker will take his men into town. If you go back to your stables, me to my rooms over Paulson's place, we're vulnerable; they'll know exactly where we are, we'll be separated, and they can take us at any time. If we're still alive when tonight's over and done with, we need distance between us and them. If they come after us now we're outnumbered, and against those odds I want an advantage. The only way we can get that is by fighting from cover.'

'A long speech, and I don't like any of it too much,' Long said.

'That's fair enough, and I'm not in a position to give orders. It's your choice, Shorty – but Bowman-Laing's old place is our best bet,' Paladin said. 'I'm moving into a high room with a big window, taking my rifle and a box of shells. If he wants me, Jack Breaker's going to need an army and a battery of howitzers.'

Without waiting for a reaction, Paladin touched his horse with his heels and took it at a fast clip across the lawns towards the big house.

Paladin, though inclined to be stubborn when he got the bit between his teeth, was also an intelligent man who liked to think he would listen when a man was talking common sense.

Long caught up with him as he was about to dismount.

'Listen,' the hostler said breathlessly, 'I'd go in with you, but what about our horses? We leave them anywhere close and they're seen, they give the game away.'

Even as he spoke, the murmur of voices Paladin had heard drew closer. The outlaws had left the clearing, made their way through the fringe of flanking trees and were heading back to the mansion.

'Damn it, you're right,' Paladin said, already moving his horse towards the side of the big house. 'They're too close already. The best we can do is get behind the stables. If you can keep the horses still and quiet—'

'Can a mother soothe her bawling infant?'

The irrepressible Long was again grinning as he spurred alongside Paladin. Together they rode up the slope and across the overgrown stable yard. There the outlaws' horses proved the point Long had made: a couple of them whinnied and pawed the ground as the two men approached, the sound carrying on the still night air.

Then they were behind the old stables, shrouded in darkness, out of the saddle and leading their horses across dead leaves and pine needles, the rank smell of rotting vegetation in their nostrils. Paladin eased his horse in close to the stables' back wall, figuring that tucked in close like that they were less likely to be seen if an outlaw took a hasty glance around the corner.

Then, leaving Long to keep the animals close to the wall and silent, he walked a little way up the slope into the woods, recklessly sweeping aside branches, snapping dead-wood underfoot as he moved in deeper. He positioned himself so that, past the end of the stables and across the yard, he could see the side of the house and a section of the moonlit front lawns.

Then he waited.

Voices again. Someone laughed. Another man said what sounded like 'shut up'. Then one of the horses teth-ered in front of the stables let out a soft whicker, and Paladin knew it had heard and scented the outlaws.

A soft whistle drew his attention. He looked across at Long. The hostler had his hand cupped on his horse's muzzle. With his other he pointed at his own eyes, up at the sky, then at Paladin. It was followed by an urgent pushing motion with the palm of his hand. He was telling Paladin moonlight was filtering through the trees, and he could be seen; to get back.

He was just in time. As Paladin backed deeper into the trees the Mexican kid came around the corner of the house. His boots swished through the weeds. He crossed the yard to the horses. That put him out of sight.

Paladin listened to the clatter of boots on steps. The antebellum's front door banged open. More thumping and banging as men moved quickly up stairs, in and out of rooms. Within minutes they were down the stairs and out again and clattering down the columned portico's steps. Two of them came around the house into the yard, carrying blanket rolls, chasing moon-cast shadows. The big man, behind him Bushwhack Jack Breaker, Brad Corrigan's marshal's badge a tarnished gleam on his vest.

I could kill him now, Paladin thought. *One shot. Make up for failing old Brad. The Mex' kid did the shooting, but plugging Breaker, the* honcho, *would likely put an end to this whole damned mess. . . .*

He eased his six-gun from its holster and lifted it high, rested the barrel on his left forearm and took a bead on Breaker. And again he was too slow, because one half of his brain was telling him to pull the trigger while the other was warning him that this was not what had been arranged with Long; that killing Breaker wouldn't tell him what five outlaws were doing moving in, executing three fine citizens, taking over the town of La Belle Commune.

Then Breaker and the big man, too, were out of sight. That put three of the outlaws with the horses – but what were the other two doing?

There was a rattle of hoofs. Wasting no time, Breaker and the big man came into view. They spurred across the yard. The sound of hoofs was muffled as the two men crossed the lawns and headed towards the bridge across the creek and so to the trail into town.

Something was wrong – but what? Paladin shifted uneasily. He pouched his six-gun. A movement attracted his attention. Long was signalling. When Paladin looked at him, this time the hostler pointed to his own nostrils, then spread both hands.

And suddenly Paladin was aware of a muted crackling,

the acrid smell of smoke.

The Mexican appeared around the edge of the stables. He was in the saddle, leading two horses. As he crossed the yard the last two men came running from the house. There was a brief exchange of words. It included, Paladin guessed, a couple of coarse comments, for the Mexican tilted his head and laughed, then flicked the reins and released their horses. The two men mounted quickly and lit out in pursuit of Breaker and the big outlaw.

The Mexican hung back. His horse turned, backed, danced a little with long tail flicking, and the kid grinned and held the reins high, his white teeth flashing. He looked straight at where Paladin was hiding, raised a fore-finger, pointed it like a pistol.

'If it is your intention to hide in the woods, my friend, you should maybe blacken your big shiny six-gun,' he called. 'One idea is to hold it over a fire for the coating of soot, you understand?' He flicked a thumb over his shoulder. 'Me and Breaker, we think that, so we give you some help. You want a fire, you have a big one any minute now. It is a pity about the house, but we have finished with it anyway, and the old woman, she will soon be dead. Possibly.'

He shrugged his shoulders, spread his hands eloquently, and with another grin he had spun his horse and was away across the lawns.

'Why didn't you plug him?' Long said bitterly, coming away from the stable wall with the horses. 'He was on his own and talking fit to bust. If you'd winged him we could've got the story out of him, found out what these fellers are up to.'

'Too late for regrets,' Paladin said. 'But what about the house?'

Even as he spoke, as smoke whipped across his face and brought tears to his eyes, he knew it was a question with only one answer.

Emma Bowman-Laing's antebellum mansion was doomed. The encircling trees shielded it from strong seasonal winds, but created a sun trap. Over the years the timber construction had dried out in the blistering heat of long summers. The fire started by the outlaws was ripping through it with frightening speed.

'Done for,' Long said, answering the question as they mounted and moved away from the yard to watch in disbelief from the moonlit cool of the lawns. 'To put that out'd take a chain of men with buckets bringing water from the creek – and they'd be wasting their time.'

'Which is what we're doing watching it die,' Paladin said. 'Three men have been shot. Mac and Rik are in the woods. Brad went in the creek, so Christ knows where he is now. It's incumbent upon us to go find him, and give all three a decent burial.'

'More than that,' Long said, turning away from the searing heat that was hitting them all the way across the lawn as brilliant tongues of flame erupted from windows and the broken roof and began licking at the trees. 'I've got a hunch Brad could be alive. Lying somewhere downstream, soaking wet, bleeding to death—'

'Rider coming,' Paladin warned, and he turned his horse to face the Bowman-Laing bridge.

SIX

Grey smoke from the burning building was being flattened by an unusual down draught and driven in a south-westerly direction across the lawns. Inexplicably, that down draught was beating back the flames. It seemed to Paladin that though much of the building would be destroyed, a shell would remain. There would be stairs leading to blackened floors, rafters where once there had been a roof. . . .

Then those thoughts were pushed out of Paladin's head by the more pressing problem of the approaching rider. Choking, eyes streaming, he and Long rode back towards the trees on the eastern side of the land. There they turned. Long cocked the Henry rifle, rested it across his thighs.

What had alerted Paladin had been a horse's soft snorting and the jingle of harness. Now, burning eyes squinting, he saw it. Very softly, he said, 'Jesus Christ, Shorty.'

Alongside him, Long said, 'And Amen to that,' and he let the hammer down on the cartridge and slipped the rifle into its boot.

Emma Bowman-Laing on her chestnut mare had emerged from the drifting smoke like a mythical knight riding out of Arthurian mists. A man was seated behind her. His arms were around her waist and he was clinging on with fingers like claws. His long legs were dangling, and from his boots fell glittering drops of water. The flickering yellow flames turned them into droplets of shimmering liquid gold, but from his arms other drops were falling, and they were bright red.

With another soft curse, Paladin rode to meet the widow and her burden as she drew rein. He swung his horse around and rode in until he was stirrup to stirrup with the chestnut; was vaguely aware of Long doing the same on the other side.

'Brad?' Paladin put a hand on the marshal's arm, shook it gently. The shirt was cold, and soaking wet. Blood was seeping down through the wet clothing from a wound high on his shoulder, dripping from his bent elbow.

'He's out,' Bowman-Laing said. 'I imagine his fingers have locked and that's all that's stopping him from falling.'

'Where did you find him?'

'I saw him go in the creek with a splash. I'd already moved a little way upstream from the bridge because when bullets are flying there's always the chance of a wild one, or a ricochet. Brad had grabbed hold of a trailing branch and clung on. He looked up, saw me peering down at him. The bullet had hit him hard, but the shock of the ice cold water kept him from passing out. He raised a hand, waggled in the way that says wait, wait. . . So I did, and, when it was safe to do so, I crossed over the bridge and he was lying in the grass. He'd managed to crawl out of the creek.'

'They carried another man into the trees. He was the second, so I'd say the two of them are there, Mackie and Paulson.'

She nodded, her mouth a thin line. 'Like Brad, they were shot in the back.'

While talking, Paladin was running his hands over Brad Corrigan's body, searching for more wounds. There was just the one. Just one of Rodriguez's bullets had caught him in the shoulder as he ran for the creek. So far nothing had been done to stem the bleeding. Paladin reached up, slipped loose his bandanna, began folding it into a thick pad.

'Mackie and Rik Paulson both dead,' he said softly. He was pushing the wadded bandanna inside Brad's wet shirt, over the ugly bullet wound. He sensed Bowman-Laing watching him and said, 'You did well getting Brad here, Emma. How'd you manage his dead weight?'

'He was still conscious – just. I helped him up on to the bridge, made him stand there, then rode my horse into the water so he could come down on to the horse rather than climb up – which he couldn't have managed.'

'That was quick thinking,' Long said, 'but now he needs a doctor – and fast. Forbes—'

'Yes, and presently you can go and drag that cantankerous old sawbones out of bed,' Bowman-Laing said, 'but first we get Brad settled; out of those clothes, dry, somewhere warm, and I need both of you for that.'

'You've got us,' Paladin said, 'but once you saw your old house going up in flames you'd have been better off heading back to town. Now there's all that way to go back, and with Brad bleeding like a stuck pig, well. . . .'

They were talking above the hiss and crackle of the fire that was now noticeably dying. Bowman-Laing seemed indifferent to what was happening to her old home. She twisted her neck, tried to look over her shoulder at Brad. He was flat against her back, his cheek turned against her shoulder like a man comfortably asleep, but his closed eyes seemed deeply sunken in a face like old wet snow and his nostrils were flaring at every ragged intake of breath.

'No, town's out if we want this feller to make it,' Bowman-Laing said. 'And you're right, I did see the fire; saw it, smelt it, shed an angry tear – but it made no difference because that wasn't where I was heading.'

'Then where?' Paladin began, but he was cut off by Bowman-Laing.

'Follow me,' she said. Without haste, one elbow clamped on Corrigan's embracing arm to hold him more firmly in place, she got the chestnut moving and headed out of the ragged fringes of drifting smoke and straight into the trees on the east side of the house.

'My grandaddy called it a hunting lodge,' Emma Bowman-Laing said. 'You must have heard me mention it earlier. He never did any hunting in his life, only thing he ever shot dead was a runaway slave. But he liked the sound of the name, told his highfalutin friends all about it, his words considerably embellished with imagined deeds.'

It was a log cabin buried in the woods, reached by the little-used trail Paladin and Long had followed in the widow's wake. Tangled undergrowth snagged their clothing and drew snorting protests from the horses. Then, after ten minutes negotiating the trail as it twisted and turned and climbed ever higher, moonlight filtering through the trees had revealed a shingle roof through which a stone chimney jutted, the pale shine of walls of peeled logs.

They caught up with the widow as she pulled the chestnut to a halt by a sagging hitch rail, moved in to hold the unconscious marshal while she dismounted and opened the door, then carried him inside. Within minutes Emma and Paladin had him stripped naked and in bed in the single back room, his body warming under a heap of soft animal skins.

By then Shorty Long was gone, hammering back the way they had come and then on down to a house on the outskirts of town occupied by a man called Forbes who had, once upon a time, been a good doctor.

'I was going to ask you how you came to be there when Brad needed you,' Paladin said, coming back into the bedroom with two steaming tin cups of coffee. 'I think I know the answer. If I'm right, then you saw everything.'

'Saw everything,' Bowman-Laing said, 'but didn't follow you from town if that's what you mean. I rode up the short way, snuck into the woods on the west side of my grandaddy's bridge. Watched the moon come up. Watched them herd Brad and the others down from the house, shoot Mackie and Rik Paulson and haul them off into the woods.' she smiled. 'Saw you plug that outlaw, and it was all I could do not to scream with joy.' Her smile faded, and she shook her head. 'I watched Brad make a run for it with my pulse hammering and my heart in my mouth.' She stopped, looked with despair at the bed, at the man who was now taking one ragged breath and pausing for far too long before the next. 'I saw cold-blooded murder committed, Paladin,' she said brokenly, 'and did nothing.'

'Nothing?' Paladin shook his head. 'That's wrong, and you know it. Brad's alive now because of your quick thinking.'

'But two men are dead.' She looked at him pleadingly, her eyes moist. 'What's it all about, Paladin?'

'Money. Has to be. For men like that, outlaws, killers, it's the only motive.'

'Damn it, you know that can't be right. In La Belle Commune, there is no money.'

'There must be. Somewhere.'

Very softly, Bowman-Laing said, 'I furnished this lodge with one or two items from the house. Nowadays I come here much more frequently, because in here with the door open wide and the sunlight slanting down through the trees I'm once again a lady of means. For a little while I can convince myself I'm not being dragged down by what confronts and offends me every day in La Belle Commune. Paladin, there is no money in La Belle Commune.'

'If the money's not there now,' Paladin said doggedly, 'then. . . .' He shook his head irritably, baffled, unable to take his thoughts further.

'If it's not there now, this money,' she said, watching him, 'it must be coming in from outside, and pretty soon. Is that it? They know something, those outlaws? They're here because . . . because what? Government money's on it's way, bullion, a wagon heading for La Belle Commune but bound for Lord knows where? That would be a first in my lifetime. Or is it something else, something we—?'

Paladin had stopped her with a raised hand. His pulse had quickened. His scalp prickled. He was remembering the man riding at an easy pace through La Belle Commune, Bushwhack Jack Breaker with the moustache and dusty flat-crowned black hat and his quick smile and inordinate interest when he spotted the track known as Salty's Notch.

Which led arrow-straight to the waters of the Gulf of Mexico.

'A boat,' Paladin said softly.

'Oh, of course,' Bowman-Laing murmured with mock approval, 'the Spanish Main, pirates and their stolen hordes of silver pieces of eight. Your imagination, Paladin, is quite breathtaking.'

And from the bed a halting voice said weakly, 'To figure out what this Breaker's up to . . . that's what it takes, imagination . . . or a bullet in the back.'

The chuckle was strained but genuine. Corrigan was white-faced and drawn but supporting himself on one elbow. He managed a grin when Bowman-Laing sprang to his bedside. 'I've got the one, Paladin the other,' he said, touching her cheek with fingers that trembled, 'so I reckon between us we can finish them off.'

SEVEN

By an hour after sunrise the next day, Bushwhack Jack Breaker was behind the desk in Brad Corrigan's office. Lomax and Flint had been sent to the western end of town. Flint was a man with a sharp mind and a temperament that was always ice-cold. He would control the gun-crazy Lomax, or use him as he saw fit. Their orders were to stop anyone entering the town. Breaker was certain the men meeting the elder Rodriguez would come in from that direction, from Texas. So, although he'd called their taking of La Belle Commune a lock-down, he wasn't particularly concerned about its eastern flank.

Meanwhile, in town, Devlin was making his menacing presence highly visible. A powerful man holding the reins of his strong bay gelding in huge fists, he rode up the street giving the blank windows in the scattering of ramshackle houses on both sides the evil eye. People seeing him, Breaker reckoned, would back off and keep their heads down. Batten down the hatches, the outlaw thought with a grin. Now, wouldn't that be an appropriate way of putting it, in the circumstances?

Rodriguez was with Breaker. The smoke from the young Mexican's cigarillo was curling in the shafts of sunlight, moved by the draught from the open window. He was standing, twirling his red and yellow sombrero in his slim hands. His smile was always there, lurking.

'Listen, kid,' Breaker said, 'I'm asking you again, have you got this right? The boat comes in tonight?'

'They are annoying, these questions. I have told you six, maybe seven times.'

'And I've been listening, but something about this deal stinks to high heaven. I mean, why the hell are you selling your brother down the river? He's bringing in a heap of cash. You and he would be rich men. Why tell me and the others?'

'There has always been bad feeling between us. I am younger. In the *pueblo*, he treat me badly, most days. So now I get even, take the money and run.' His white teeth glinted. 'Leave him dead on the beach, maybe.'

Breaker was leaning back, smoking. His eyes were thoughtful.

'You told me several men would be meeting your brother. Is that why you're not one of them? Because of this bad blood?'

'Is ridiculous, that thought. We have not spoken for several years. I learn of this amazing thing he has done, this fortune he has stolen, from a person I cannot name.'

'Well,' Breaker said, 'if these men are coming they're cutting it fine.'

'Several men with a buckboard, or maybe one man with a spare horse, which would be sufficient.' Rodriguez shrugged. 'In my mind I am not certain of the facts, but it is of no consequence. They will arrive. Flint and Lomax will be there waiting. In my opinion they must shoot them very dead.'

'All taken care of,' Breaker said, and he swung out of the chair and poured himself a cup of coffee. He turned to watch Rodriguez walk out into the street, and had the cup raised to his lips when the first distant shots crackled.

The buckboard came rattling in from the direction of the Texas border. Its plume of brown dust drifted across the flat land bordering the blue waters of the Gulf of Mexico, discolouring the thin white mist and shimmering heat-haze. The trail was rough and little used, making the long ride uncomfortable for the three men on the buckboard's hard seats. They were sore, hot and sweating. Travelling due west, they'd been forced to squint ahead into the daz-zling glare of the early morning sun. It was little wonder, Flint thought, that there was relief on the driver's glisten-ing face when he pulled the wagon to a halt.

Flint was out in the middle of the trail, his hand raised. Gun pouched. Nothing in his manner to suggest trouble. Or theirs, but that would change, and quickly. He had little doubt that these were the men meeting Alvaro Rodriguez. Lazily, he wondered what the reaction would be when he told them that they could go no further.

At the same time, the animal instinct that had many times saved his life in the past was telling him that some-thing was badly wrong.

'Bad news, fellers,' he said. 'Or maybe you should look on it as good news: this is as far as you go.'

A big man jumped down, stretched, scratched the

damp back of his neck. He had a paunch, keen eyes, a six-gun he shifted on his hip without taking his eyes from Flint.

'You mind clarifying?'

'Fever. Real bad, it's killing folk indiscriminately.' Flint smiled at that; thought of it as him and the big man bat-tling with big words they maybe didn't understand. 'My job is to keep the town locked down,' he said, 'until the medics from New Orleans give the OK.'

'And if it's not the town we want, but the beach?'

'That's like choosing where to die,' Flint said. 'There' – he jerked a thumb towards the Gulf – 'or here.'

'Here?' The big man's eyebrow lifted. He glanced away to his left, to where two horses were tethered alongside a patch of dense scrub thirty yards to the north of the trail. 'We ain't set foot in town yet. You telling me you're infected. You and your friend over there?'

'What I'm telling you,' Flint said, 'is to turn that goddamn buckboard around and get the hell of of here.'

The big man sighed, puffing his cheeks out.

'Christ, are you listening to this?' he said, talking side-ways to the two men in the buckboard but watching Flint with an amused smile.

'You want I should run him down,' the driver said.

'I can do better than that, and faster,' the big man said, and he went for his gun.

He got his hand to the butt and was lifting the big Colt when the shot cracked. Smoke puffed from the patch of scrub. It was short range for a long gun. The big man took the bullet from Lomax's rifle in the side of the jaw. Blood and bone splinters flew in a spray, glistening red in the sun. He went down in a heap, rolled face down. His legs twitched. One hand flapped feebly at his face.

The second shot sent the driver's hat flying. He ducked down, then grabbed a shotgun from under the seat and rolled out of the buckboard. The man sitting immediately behind him had a steely glint in his eyes. His six-gun was out and cocked. He stayed where he was, squinting into the sun; waiting, when waiting was to invite sudden death.

He was lucky. Lomax chose that moment to lower the rifle and break cover. The man in the buckboard dropped him with a single shot; a long shot for a handgun. Before the crack of the pistol had faded, from under the wagon the shotgun blasted. It tore Lomax's face to bloody shreds as he crumpled.

'Pretty fair shooting,' Flint said, in a conversational tone, 'but don't say I didn't warn you.'

He dropped to one knee and killed the man under the wagon with two fast shots. The dying man's finger tightened on the scattergun's second trigger. The blast hit the wheels and buckshot whined away in the hot air.

The man in the buckboard sprang upright. He spun to face Flint. His six-gun was up and cocked. He turned fast, but, against a man like Flint his fastest turn would always have been too slow. He'd made it halfway round when a bullet took him in the throat. A second punched a black hole between his eyes. He fell across the seat. The six-gun clattered, dropped on to the dusty trail. In the sudden silence Flint could clearly hear blood from the terrible throat wound dripping on the boards.

He looked towards Lomax. Thought about the damage a shotgun inflicts, and shook his head. Deakin downed by the house, now Lomax. Five reduced to three, and with a thin smile he thought of how the gold would be divvied. Then he turned his gaze on the three dead men. They were not what he'd expected. Outlaws live on their nerves. Most are unshaven to present a tough image, hungry most of the time. Flint couldn't remember seeing one with a padding of fat.

He walked towards the big man, the man with a paunch downed by Lomax, and dropped to one knee. The man was stone dead, his hand on his shattered face. With an effort Flint flopped him on to his back, and grimaced. Shattered bone, sticky with blood, caked in dust. He was wearing a cowhide vest. In the top pocket, Flint found a badge. He stood up, leaned back against the buckboard. The badge was cupped in his hand. He slipped it into his pocket, fashioned a cigarette, scraped a match and blew a stream of smoke.

He figured there was no point searching the other men. The instinct that had warned him something was wrong left him in no doubt: all three men who had arrived to meet the boat carrying Alvaro Rodriguez and his stolen gold were badged US marshals.

EIGHT

'There were three of them, in a buckboard,' Paladin said. 'Two of the outlaws were waiting. Some talk went back and forth I wasn't close enough to hear. Whatever was said it led to a gunfight. When the dust settled the only man left standing was that lean, black-clad outlaw.'

'Flint,' Shorty Long said. 'That's his name.'

'How'd you know that?'

'The widow rode down with me. I did some chores in the stables. Next thing I know I'm out in the sun and she's standing outside the jail talking to that Mexican kid and Bushwhack Jack Breaker.'

'The devil you say.'

Long grinned. 'Had that crazy yellow parasol. I could hear her tinkling laugh. She was disarming them with an old lady's charm, playing innocent but missing nothing.'

Paladin had been a keen observer of the gunfight from a low rise some fifty yards back from the thick patch of scrub. When he'd seen enough he'd ridden away fast and hard, making damn sure the remaining outlaw knew he'd been watched. But knowing Breaker and the Mexican were in Brad's jail, he had circled high above the town and come into Long's stables by the back way.

'I think the three men in the buckboard,' Paladin said now, 'were lawmen.'

The hostler's eyes narrowed. 'But you're not sure?'

'Flint searched one of them. Stood up with something glittering in his hand. Seemed a mite put out. Stood smoking, glancing down every now and then at what he'd found.'

'You reckon these lawmen were after Breaker?'

'No.'

'Then what?'

Paladin shook his head. 'I don't know.'

'The widow's gone back to the lodge. She called here briefly when she'd done with her work as a spy. My guess is she learned a whole lot more than she told me in that time.'

'Then let's go find out,' Paladin said.

From observing the little hostler Paladin knew that weariness must be writ naked across his own countenance when they walked into the lodge.

It had been well past midnight when Long returned with the town's drunken doctor, Nathan Forbes. Though bleary eyed and stinking of strong drink, the mumbling old man had dressed Corrigan's bullet wound with skill and tenderness. When he rode back to town on a horse that looked half blind he carried with him a silver dollar from Bowman-Laing, and the memory of her kiss on his flushed, lined cheek.

Corrigan slept. Emma dozed in her chair by the bed.

Paladin had lowered the lamp and taken Long and a couple of rusty spades and together they had traipsed across the slope to the woods. There they had stripped to their undershirts, and with the sounds of night birds and the nearby creek in their ears had dug shallow graves in ground criss-crossed with roots. After an hour's back-breaking work, they had buried the bodies of their two friends.

The skies had been lightening with approaching dawn when they smoothed the last of the red soil and laid a covering of dead leaves. They had tried to grab an hour's sleep in the lodge's living room. Long snored for a while, but Paladin's active mind kept him awake. For the first time since he'd last walked out of Paulson's place, he felt the craving for hard liquor.

'I was wrong, last night,' Brad Corrigan said.

His voice was much stronger. The marshal was lying back in a comfortable chair close to the living-room's window, stripped to the waist, bandages a pure white in the slanting sunlight and his feet up on a wooden stool. 'I said imagination and a bullet in the back would see us through,' he went on. 'What I neglected to mention was the intelligence and fearlessness of this fine woman.'

'Actually it was all down to luck, and playing on the pre-conceived notions of stupid men,' Bowman-Laing said. 'It's surprising how the need for caution is forgotten when an old dear like me's dismissed as senile. Breaker had a good idea who I was, of course, from my riding past the house that time. He still didn't see the danger. They plopped me down in a chair with a cup of strong coffee to

revive me after the strain of my walk, then left me to doze'
– she smiled – 'or die. They went outside, lit cigarettes,
stood in the hot sun. And they talked; they kept their
voices low – they had some sense – but the door was open
and I have sharp ears. That Mexican boy's full of himself.
He spilled most of the beans – in his case I suppose that
should be frijoles – and when after a while I walked away
with deliberate unsteadiness and a vague look in my eyes,
I had most of the story.'

'I figured a boat,' Paladin said. 'You scoffed at the very
idea.'

'But you were right,' Emma said. 'It comes in tonight.
The Mexican boy's brother's on board, one Alvaro
Rodriguez. He's the man with the money we were wondering about – whether it's gold or banknotes isn't clear.
He stole it somewhere in South America, and trekked his
way north. He's got men meeting him here. They're
coming in from Texas.'

Paladin was frowning. 'Why? Breaker and his men are
here with this Alvaro's brother.'

'Who is out for some kind of revenge. Somehow he
heard of Alvaro's sudden riches, doesn't care much for
him, and hit on the idea of taking the money.'

'Someone else got wind of that faraway theft,' Shorty
Long said. He looked at Paladin. 'If you were right, those
lawmen were here not to arrest Breaker, but to put the
handcuffs on Alvaro Rodriguez.'

'I think it's more complicated,' Paladin said. 'What if
Rodriguez is already in irons. Say he was caught when he
was setting sail—'

'From Vera Cruz,' Bowman-Laing said.

'—and is now a prisoner. Wires hummed, signals went back and forth, and he's to be handed over to Texas lawmen meeting the boat.'

'What damn Texas lawmen?' Brad Corrigan said. 'I've been listening and not following one damn word.'

'They've been dealt with, and Breaker's lost another man,' Paladin said. 'There are no men coming in from Texas to help Alvaro Rodriguez. Tonight, young Rodriguez will be down there on the shore looking for a light flashing out at sea. He'll acknowledge it. A small boat will come in, and the kid thinks he's going to grab the cash from his brother. If I'm right, Alvaro is in irons, there'll be an armed escort, and Breaker and the Mexican kid are looking at one hell of a battle.'

'Leave 'em to it,' Brad Corrigan said bluntly. 'By dawn they'll all be out of here.'

'Leaving two good men buried in the woods,' Bowman-Laing pointed out.

'Something we cannot forget,' Paladin said, 'and that makes one more score I've got to settle with Bushwhack Jack Breaker.' He grinned coldly. 'Come dark tonight, there'll be more horses passing through Salty's Notch than through a bronc chute on rodeo day.'

The former wrangler and bronc buster chuckled. 'My word, that takes me back.' And then he sobered. 'Emma's made the point, and you reinforced it: the killing of Mackie and Paulson cannot go unpunished. But what's your plan, Paladin? I take it we're going down there tonight, but when we get there – then what?'

'I don't know,' Paladin said. 'But as a bounty hunter, that's been the story of my life.'

NINE

Bloody-minded, flatly refusing to take no for an answer, Brad Corrigan insisted on riding out with Paladin and Long. Bowman-Laing, a slim figure outlined by lamplight flooding from the doorway, was shaking her head in disbelief as she watched the two men help La Belle Commune's wounded marshal up on to his horse.

Yet, despite losing the argument with Corrigan, Paladin knew there was more. He was up against kindred spirits. Bowman-Laing had calmly told them she would remain in the lodge and wait for news. Not for one moment did Paladin believe her.

One stroke of good fortune: there was no moon. High clouds had floated in to give thin cover that created luminosity, flattening contours, turning men into pallid ghosts riding phantom horses. Knowing that Breaker, Rodriguez and the two remaining gunmen would be watching the waters of the Gulf intently from the patch of shore at the end of Salty's Notch, Paladin nevertheless chose a route that carried them wide of the town.

They crossed the trail well to the east of La Belle

Commune, going across singly. Long, holding his loaded Henry rifle across his thighs, led the way after a quick glance to ensure they were unobserved. The low ridge that in town was cut by Salty's Notch had at this point flattened to level ground, and once across the trail the horses trotted without sound across soft sandy soil. Ahead of them, black silhouettes in the wan light, the tall palm trees bordering the shore were like gallows awaiting the arrival of doomed men, the rustling of their fronds like the flutter of vultures' wings.

The three men maintained their spacing. Corrigan was a few yards behind Long, not comfortable in the saddle. Paladin took up the rear. Deliberately, he dropped back – and at once wondered what that was for, what primitive instinct was causing his scalp to prickle, the cold sweat to break out on his brow.

Long was through the palms now and on the shingle beach, Corrigan closing up. Then, behind those two men and to one side there was movement where there should have been none. Peering into the deep shadows under the palms, Paladin swore softly and reached for his six-gun. His mouth was open to call a warning when a rider pulled out. His black attire had rendered him all but invisible. He fell in behind Corrigan. Something was said that Paladin was too far away to hear. Then light glinted on the man's six-gun. It was levelled at Brad Corrigan's back. Paladin heard a hammer being cocked, followed by an icy chuckle.

The man was Flint. For Paladin, yet again, it was too late.

'There,' Breaker said softly. 'You see it – or am I going

crazy with looking?'

'There is a light, for certain,' Guillermo Rodriguez said. 'I have been watching it for several minutes. Now, I am sure. The signal is as arranged.'

'About damn time,' Breaker said, and he walked away impatiently, kicking at the shingle; turned, looked at where Devlin was standing by the palms with the three horses; looked again at the young Mexican who, to Breaker's chagrin, had been calling all the shots.

The killing of Lomax by the men in the buckboard did not concern Breaker; like Flint, he was looking forward to a welcome increase in his share of the stolen gold. However, the fact that Lomax had been gunned down by US marshals was completely unexpected. The lawmen had hinted that they had no interest in the town. '*If it's not the town we want, but the beach*', they'd said, and so the clear inference to be drawn was they were there to arrest Alvaro Rodriguez.

If they'd got wind of the stolen gold, the identity of the thief and his destination, who else knew? And where were the men Guillermo Rodriguez had said would be there to meet his brother?

Rodriguez, impatient, called, 'You have the lamp?'

Devlin came jogging across the shingle. He handed the shiny tin lantern to Rodriguez. A match flared. The lamp's wick sputtered, then caught. The yellow light was a pool wavering around the Mexican's boots as he walked down to the water's edge. He held the lantern high and swept off his sombrero. He used the big hat to cover the light, expose it, cover it again. The movements were erratically spaced.

Breaker shook his head. 'How the hell will they see that?' he growled, moving to Rodriguez' shoulder.

'It is possible even without glasses. They are close now, but only as close as is safe for a big boat. You see? Against the horizon? It is a ketch. A small boat will be lowered—'

He broke off because a distant splash told its own story.

'And now what we have been waiting for begins to happen.' Rodriguez's grin was wide and dazzling.

All three men stood peering across the flat waters with aching eyes, straining their ears. It was the kid who was first to see the small boat bringing Alvaro Rodriguez to the shore, Breaker, moments later, picking up the splash of the oars. Then they could all see it: the phosphorescence as the oars lifted dripping from the water drawing their gaze, their eyes immediately identifying the dark shape low in the water.

'Small row boat with three men,' Breaker said. 'One's working those oars. One's standing, got his hand on the other feller's shoulder.'

Rodriguez shrugged. 'Two men, three men, it is something I do not understand but it is unimportant.'

He'd placed the lantern on the shingle. Now he moved away from Breaker and Devlin, all his attention on the boat. There were no waves. The sea was lapping the shingle gently, ebbing and flowing with a faint hiss. Then, almost magically, the high cloud cover broke and the small boat was caught in a shaft of moonlight. There was a grating sound as the prow grounded, and the tall man who was on his feet lurched forward. The oars were shipped. The rower straightened, eased the kinks out of his back. The tall man bent to grasp the gunwales with one hand and stepped out into the shallow water.

The seated man rose and followed him. Dark-skinned, he wore a fancy sombrero, a neat black jacket with its edges trimmed with braid. He splashed awkwardly into the water. His hands were in front of him, his movement restricted by manacles gleaming on his wrists. As he entered the water he staggered backwards. This took him a little way away from the tall man. He bumped against the boat. It rocked. The oarsman cursed and grabbed the gunwales.

Alvaro Rodriguez flashed a glance towards his brother. Their eyes met. Guillermo Rodriguez gave an almost imperceptible nod.

And, as the tall man snapped a command at his prisoner, the night air was ripped apart by a rapid burst of distant gunfire.

TEN

Brad Corrigan fell off his horse.

To his dying day, Paladin would marvel at the wounded marshal's quick thinking. He'd heard the metallic cocking of the six-gun. The man holding the gun was behind him. Corrigan was in too much pain to twist in the saddle. He had already taken one bullet in the back. A second would surely finish him off.

So fast was Corrigan's fall, so unexpected, Flint was for a fleeting few seconds, incapable of movement. He was a man holding a cocked six-gun, pointing it at a horse without a rider.

He was snapped out of his daze by Shorty Long. The little hostler was lame in one leg but could near as dammit make a horse talk. He heard the click of a hammer followed by Brad hitting the sandy ground with a thud and a grunt of pain. With the touch of one knee and a light tug on the opposite rein Long had his horse halfway around before Flint could react. The rifle was still flat across Long's thighs. Without lifting it he jacked a shell into the breech and pulled the trigger.

In the faint moonlight the muzzle flash was blinding. The bullet plucked at Flint's empty leather holster, then sliced across his horse's rump. The animal squealed in pain, reared, hoofs flashing. Grabbing the saddle horn with one hand, firing blind, Flint managed to send three quick shots hissing out high over the Gulf. Then he tumbled backwards out of the saddle. His horse bolted, galloping towards the wide expanse of beach.

Caught well back up the trail, Paladin spurred his horse and moved in fast. Corrigan was doing his best to crawl into the shelter of the palm trees. Long had slid from his horse and was limping towards Flint. The outlaw, winded by his fall, was struggling to rise. Shocked, bruised, disorientated, he had kept his grip on his six-gun. Long, coming at him, was outlined against the luminous skies.

Flint hit him with a single shot. The hostler lurched sideways. All his weight was taken by his gammy leg. It collapsed under him and he went down in a crumpled heap.

Then Brad Corrigan rolled on to his back. Upper body raised, he gripped his Colt in both hands. Then, firing between his feet, he opened up with blazing gunfire from under the trees. At the same time Paladin leaped from his horse, dropped to one knee and triggered his six-gun.

He heard the thump of the marshal's bullets hitting flesh and bone. Saw his own bullets punch holes in the outlaw's face. Flint cried out once, pitifully. Then he flopped down, a slack body lying in the dust, devoid of life.

Silence. The distant lapping of the sea, the rustle of the palms.

'Shoulder,' Long moaned, sitting cross-legged and rocking. The rifle was still clutched in one hand. With the other he was struggling to staunch the flow of blood from the wound. 'Plugged me in the shoulder, damn him.'

'Went in the front, so at least you can reach yours,' Corrigan growled. 'Me, I hit the ground hard. The wound in my back's opened up again and there's damn all I can do about it.'

'I blame myself for what's happened,' Paladin said. 'Both of you need Doc Forbes, and this time it's my turn to go fetch him.'

Once again disgusted with his performance, he was turning his horse to go for the doctor when, from the other end of the beach, there came a rattle of gunfire.

Breaker had sent Flint out to cover the far end of the beach because he'd grown increasingly suspicious about an old woman's motives. Earlier that day she had walked into the jail looking for Corrigan. She said her name was Emma Bowman-Laing and, like most elderly folk, she had difficulty sleeping. At some time around midnight, she said sweetly, she had distinctly heard gunfire up near her old home and was rather worried.

Breaker, his mind on the crackle of gunfire coming from the outskirts of town where he'd placed his men on guard, had pacified her, taken her hand when she politely welcomed him as the new town marshal and smiled through his impatience. Then, with Rodriguez, he had stepped out into the heat of the sun and the Mex kid had never stopped talking.

Bowman-Laing, when she eventually emerged from the office and walked off up the street, had looked frail and confused. Later, Breaker was to remember her eyes, their clear bright blue and the look of intelligence in them she was unable to hide. And he wondered if she was playing him like a fish.

Now, he was again being distracted by the rattle of gunfire. Instinctively, he and Devlin turned to gaze up the stretch of beach. They looked away only fleetingly, but it was enough for Guillermo Rodriguez.

The Mexican drew his six-gun. He shot Devlin through the heart. The big man had not hit the ground before Rodriguez plucked another six-gun from his waistband and tossed it across the narrow stretch of water to his brother. Alvaro caught it deftly in his manacled hands. The tall man had also been looking along the beach. Out of the corner of his eye he caught the glint of metal as the six-gun whirled through the air. His eyes widened. He dropped his hand in a desperate attempt to draw his gun. Without hesitation Rodriguez smashed a savage blow across the bridge of his nose with the gun's barrel. Bone cracked. Blood sprayed. With a splash, the man fell face down in the water.

Moving fast, Alvaro Rodriguez tucked the six-gun in his waistband, reached back into the boat for a bulging leather case, then waded two steps forward. He drove a booted foot hard down on the tall man's back. Then he straightened his leg, leaned his weight on it and held him beneath the surface. For a few moments there was a frenzied thrashing. The man's legs kicked the water to foam stained red with his blood. Then the kicking slowed, stopped. Bubbles broke the water's surface in one brief burst, then they too died.

With a wild splashing the sailor who had ferried the

lawman and his prisoner from the ketch, dug his oars into the water, executed a hurried turn and pulled rapidly away from the shore.

And all this time Breaker was staring into the muzzle of Guillermo Rodriguez's six-gun.

'I was wrong about you,' Breaker said. 'This meeting was arranged. You didn't sell your brother down the river.'

'But it was a good story,' Guillermo Rodriguez said, grinning. 'The long ride in a wagon from Nicaragua with stolen gold with always the fear of pursuit, Alvaro's ability to sail a boat well in all weathers. But, of course, there was no wagon journey, and there is no gold. My brother, he robbed a bank in Vera Cruz.'

'And got away,' Alvaro Rodriguez said, splashing out of the shallows. 'But only for a little while and, when I knew capture was inevitable I arranged for Guillermo to meet me here. I suggested he bring men with him who would, if necessary, kill the several lawmen who would be accompanying me.' He shrugged. 'But of course there was only the one lawman, and I have myself killed him very easily.'

He had the heavy leather case in one hand. The six-gun was in the other. He had not yet fired a shot. His eyes, when he looked at Breaker, had a blank look in them Breaker knew meant his life was hanging by a thread.

'There's a lot of men dead,' Breaker said. 'Your kid brother was responsible for four of 'em.' He shook his head ruefully at Guillermo Rodriguez. 'You think that makes you some kind of red-hot gunslinger, but you had it easy, Guillermo. Three you shot in the back; Devlin, there, he was distracted; you shot a man who was looking the other way.' He paused, let the moment hang in the air then said softly, 'The odds here are two to one in your favour, but I'm looking you in the face, kid. You think you've got the guts?'

Guillermo Rodriguez took a couple of steps backwards, pouched his six-gun, held his arms out from his sides.

'Now we see,' he said. 'My brother Alvaro, he will stay out of this. It is you and me, face to face.' He grinned. 'But I think maybe you have a yellow streak, Breaker. You will run for your life and I will be forced to shoot you in the back—'

'Get it done,' Alvaro snapped, 'there's riders coming fast along the beach.'

And in that instant when Guillermo flicked a glance at his brother, Jack Breaker went for his gun. He was swift. His hand accomplished the short down-and-up movement in the blink of an eye. He curled his thumb over the hammer. The snapped upward movement cocked the heavy weapon. He was too fast for Guillermo Rodriguez. The kid's lips drew back from his gleaming white teeth. His hand touched the butt of his gun but already he was staring death in the face: the black hole of a six-gun's muzzle.

Breaker was fast, but his desperate effort was wasted because yet again Guillermo Rodriguez had lied through his teeth. In the instant before Breaker could squeeze the trigger, Alvaro lifted his six-gun casually and shot him in the arm. Breaker's fingers went dead. His six gun fell in wet sand.

Alvaro Rodriguez grabbed Guillermo's arm, pulled him away and, as hoofbeats hammered closer, the brothers sprinted for the three horses tethered under the palms.

ELEVEN

Confusion. A jumble of sounds and impressions bombarding a mind numbed by gunfire that seemed to have battered Paladin's consciousness from every imaginable direction. The close-range brittle cracks of handguns punching killing holes in the man called Flint had left his ears ringing and his senses sickened, but still he had heard that faint rattle of gunfire from the western end of the beach.

As Paladin set off to investigate, pushing his horse to a gallop, he could hear behind him faint, measured hoof-beats as Shorty Long and Brad Corrigan rode away from the beach. Both men sat unsteadily in the saddle. Riding cautiously at a pace that would not jar their wounds, they would be calling in at the doctor's house on the way back up to the lodge. This was at the insistence of Emma Bowman-Laing. The indefatigable widow had followed them down from the burnt-out shell of her antebellum home – as Paladin had known she would – had witnessed the shooting of Long and Flint and had been bitterly scathing in her comments when Corrigan emerged weak and bloodied from under the palms.

Now, despite the thunderous pounding of his own horse's hoofs on the coarse sand and the faint whisper of those behind him, Paladin could also hear hoofbeats up ahead. Those too, at first carrying clearly on the still air, were now rapidly fading. He was leaning well forward in the saddle, his hands holding the reins along the sides of his racing horse's neck. His eyes were busy, scanning every inch of the moonlit beach.

Far ahead, where the line of palms was broken by the opening of Salty's Notch, Paladin thought he saw three horses, with just two riders. Then, as suddenly as wraiths passing through a stone wall, they were gone.

The salt wind was in his face, clearing his head. The sea was flat but for a long swell, the water eerily luminous in the light of the moon. A dark smudge with pencil-thin masts cast a shadow half a mile off shore. Paladin could see the faint glimmer of the boat's running lights, and his thoughts were racing. The vessel appeared to be at anchor. The water was too shallow for it to come closer. One of the boat's crew would bring Alvaro Rodriguez and his stolen gold to the shore in a dinghy or row boat. The Mexican would be met by his brother and Bushwhack Jack Breaker. Three men. But unless Paladin's eyesight was failing, he had seen just those two mounted men and one riderless horse.

As Paladin drew level with the entrance to the Notch and pulled his horse back to a canter, the faint scent of cordite drifted to his nostrils. Almost at once he saw, midway between the palms and the sea, the inert body of a big man lying flat on his face in the sand. Close to him, another man was sitting cross legged. He wore a flat-crowned black hat. When he turned to look at Paladin his face was white, the pallor emphasized by the drooping black moustache.

Bushwhack Jack Breaker. Alone, and wounded.

'I'll live,' Breaker said. His hand was clamped to his bloody right arm, his lips tight against his teeth. 'Devlin's dead. Go tear strips off his shirt and bind this arm. Then we're going after those Mexicans.'

'We?'

'The kid Guillermo killed your three friends.'

'Two. The town marshal lived.'

'OK. But the kid shot all three in the back and two died.' Breaker's attempt at a grin was a painful grimace. 'You were a bounty hunter. You and me catch 'em, we'll split the stolen cash.'

'There's no gold?'

'It's a long story. I was taken in. What those fellers have got is a leather case stuffed with the proceeds of a Vera Cruz bank robbery.'

'Then sooner or later the law will get them.'

'It's been tried, here, in La Belle Commune. Flint and Lomax gunned down three Texas marshals.'

'And now Lomax and Flint are dead,' Paladin said.

'Ah. You got Flint?' Breaker nodded. 'Then the men I brought here are all dead except that Mex kid,' Breaker said, 'and him and his brother will give the law one hell of a run for their money.'

His choice of words caused him to grin. Then, clearly thinking of a long and difficult pursuit across Texas, he attempted a dismissive shrug of the shoulders and drew in a sharp breath through clenched teeth as pain lanced through his arm.

'What makes you think I'd ride with you anyway?' Paladin said. 'Go back, what, five or six years? I seem to remember you plugging me in the back and throwing me in the Red River to drown.'

Rocking with the pain of his wounded arm, Breaker was shaking his head.

'That was Rodriguez.'

'What, the kid? He was with you, yes, but six years ago he'd be no more than twelve years old.'

'For Christ's sake,' Breaker hissed, 'will you do something about this goddamn wound before I bleed to death?'

The dead outlaw Devlin was face down. Paladin rolled him over, ripped open his vest and dragged his shirt out of his pants. He tore off two strips. Then he used his folding knife to slash Breaker's sleeve from wrist to shoulder, and bound the bloody groove the bullet had gouged across the outlaw's upper arm muscle.

With an effort, Breaker climbed shakily to his feet. He rocked, braced himself, then took a deep breath, again shook his head.

'About Rodriguez, it was him shot you all right. Mexicans always look too damn young, or too damn old. I always called Guillermo a kid, but that kid's pushing thirty, was in his early twenties when he left you to drown.'

'But you were there.'

'I've been a lot of places, a lot of times,' Breaker said, 'and time is what we're wasting.'

PART TWO

TWELVE

Paladin and Bushwhack Jack Breaker cut south of Houston a week after crossing the Sabine River, skirting Galveston Bay and pushing their gaunt horses on to the settlement of Bay City.

Ten miles east of Houston, late afternoon, they'd stopped at an old staging post on a dusty trail along which tumbleweed skittered before the hot dry wind. A bearded man with a French accent served them with warm beer across a worm-eaten plank bar sagging between two barrels. When asked, he told them two Mexicans had passed through early that day. Eaten a meal in a hurry. A young kid with a flashing grin, an older man who was sober and reflective. Both were watching their back trail as if Indians were on the warpath with sharp scalping knives. The older man, he said, downed his ham, eggs and coffee without once entirely letting go of his worn leather case.

It was the first time the question they'd grown sick of asking had drawn the right response. They had left La Belle Commune two days after the killings on the beach, two days after the Rodriguez brothers had left town. The

101

night's gunfire had disturbed none of the residents. Shorty Long was in his rooms behind the stables. Brad Corrigan, looked after by Bowman-Laing who had no faith in the drunken doctor, Forbes, had moved back down to the jail.

'There's a spare badge in a drawer,' he'd told Paladin. 'Shinier than the one Jack Breaker stole,' he added with a grin, 'so I guess while you're away huntin' those Mexicans I'll just sit in that old rocking chair showin' off and soaking up some sun.'

Yet there had been a message lurking behind the marshal's amused gaze that presented Paladin with both a puzzle and a sense of foreboding. Corrigan, though nursing wounds, had ridden down from the lodge without too much trouble. There was, Paladin knew, nothing stopping the wily old lawman from riding much further than that if he got ideas into his head.

With that a constant worry at the back of his mind, it was little wonder that oft-times on the ride into Texas Paladin caught himself looking nervously over his shoulder.

After a couple of days on the trail, Paladin and Breaker had begun to believe they were pursuing two men who had vanished off the face of the earth. No sightings, their questions always drawing reluctant, taciturn, negative responses. Now, if the owner of the staging post could be trusted, the Rodriguez brothers had reappeared: Paladin and Breaker were closing in on their quarry.

In that week's hard riding they'd gained a day and a half, but paid the price. In Bay City, with the sun already down and shadows lengthening, they had first placed their head-hung horses in the care of the hostler in the town's only livery barn. Then sheer bone weariness had forced them to book a room in the town's only hotel, plod fifty yards to the only café and wolf down the first hot meal they'd had in days. By stopping overnight, a big chunk of the time they had gained would be lost. But, Paladin pointed out, if he and Breaker were keeping going through will-power and a bloody-minded determination not to give up, the two Mexicans could be faring no better. At some time they too would be forced to stop running.

'Peasant stock,' Paladin said, pushing away his greasy plate and sitting back with a sigh. 'For them, *mañana*'s a way of life. Now they're running for their lives, and it must be killing 'em.'

'Can't happen too soon for me,' Breaker said. His drooping moustache was flecked with egg yolk, glistening with grease. The curling smoke from his cigarette was causing his black eyes to narrow, and he was absently rubbing the healing bullet wound in his arm.

'Sit there, relax,' Paladin said, pushing back from the table. 'I'll go check on the horses, make sure they'll be fit by early tomorrow. I'll see you back at the hotel.'

He crossed the street to the livery barn with pools of light spilling into the street from hanging oil lamps, then into the big barn where horizontal beams held saddles of all kinds, and movement and the rustling of straw could be heard in most of the stalls. The sound of his boots on the hard-packed runway brought the hostler yawning out of his lighted office. He was a rangy man casting a long shadow. His bald head was tanned like old shiny leather, and deep lines like knife scars ran from each side of his bony nose.

'Nothing oats, water, a good rub down and a night's sleep won't put right,' he said in answer to Paladin's question. 'They've had the first three, now settling down to the fourth. If you can take advice, I'd say go easy on 'em. Or if you're in that much of a damned hurry, take a couple of horses so you can change mounts from time to time.' He grinned. 'It worked for the Pony Express, and I can offer a good deal on a couple of horses'll take you all the way across Texas.'

Paladin nodded. 'That's something to think on; the men we're hunting have a spare. Two Mexicans. They killed men in Louisiana, cold-blooded shootings. They're also carrying a heap of stolen cash.'

'You the law?'

'A couple of the men they murdered were friends of mine.' Paladin left it at that, paused. 'We heard from a Frenchie running a bar in an old staging post that the Mexicans were heading this way. D'you see them pass through?'

'Nope.'

'You're sure?'

'Positive.'

'You haven't seen them?'

'I didn't say that.'

Paladin rolled his eyes. 'So what the hell did you say?'

'I said I ain't seen 'em pass through. Because they ain't done that. They're still here. If they're not, they left town on foot, because that's their horses you can hear movin' about in the stalls next to yours.'

Paladin left the barn fighting considerable unease. Cautiously, he stepped out into the street, then leaned back against the big doors that were folded open against the building. They creaked under his weight. Across the street the café's window was steamed up, but Paladin could see enough to know Breaker had left. The room they'd booked in the hotel was second floor front looking down on the flimsy board covering over the gallery that stretched the full width of the building. There was a faint light in the window.

Bay City was one main street, and it was deserted but for a cowboy walking unsteadily to his horse. Across from the hotel, a little way up from the livery barn, there was a saloon. A piano was tinkling. A woman was singing, off-key. The faint smell of beer and cigarette smoke reached Paladin. He wondered if the two Mexicans were in there drinking. Thought maybe not. If they were as tired as he was, they'd have bedded down for the night. But where?

And then he allowed himself a sardonic smile because, by hell, wouldn't it be interesting if they too had booked into the only hotel in town?

For a couple of long minutes Paladin tossed mental coins, lips pursed in thought. Then, coming to a decision, he pushed himself away from the big doors and walked the short way to the low-slung stone building he'd spotted while eating his chow.

The town jail.

The door was open. He walked into a lamp-lit room that put Brad Corrigan's office in La Belle Commune to shame. A safe, two old wooden filing cabinets, a big iron pot-bellied stove. The walls were adorned with Wanted dodgers, fading prints and notes scrawled in ink or pencil on scrap paper. A cuspidor looked like solid brass and was dusty from lack of use. A gun rack held rifles that had the sheen of oil regularly applied.

There was a scarred oak roll-top desk with its back against the side wall. On it there was an ornate typewriting machine with a sheet of paper rolled in. The town marshal was sitting by the desk. He'd swivelled his chair and was watching Paladin with intelligent grey eyes. On the scattered papers by the typewriting machine a dove grey Stetson lay next to a Colt .45 which was within easy reach.

'Jim Grey,' he said softly, 'at your service. You look like a man's got troubles gnawing at his insides.'

'I'm about to get rid of them. The hostler over at the barn—'

'Johnson, by name,' the marshal said, and winked. 'Most folks call him Curly on account of all that hair.'

'He said two Mexicans rode in, left their horses with him. They're still there, so the men are still in town. They're killers, making their way home toting a leather bag full of stolen cash.'

'I don't think so.'

Paladin frowned. 'What's that mean? You're calling me a liar?'

'Take a seat,' Jim Grey said.

'I feel more like taking a swing at your chin.'

'The thing is,' Jim Grey said, 'a little after noon today those two greasers you mentioned were standing exactly where you are now, saying about you exactly what you just said about them. Told me your name, too. Paladin.' He smiled sadly. 'A man of my experience, that set some mighty loud warning bells ringing.'

And with the easy familiarity of a man who knew exactly what he was doing he picked up the Colt, pointed it at Paladin and thumbed back the hammer.

THIRTEEN

It didn't take long for Paladin to figure out that Jim Grey had reached a comfortable middle age for a town marshal by always exercising extreme caution. Just about long enough for a cell door to clang behind him and a key selected from a big jingling bunch to turn in the lock. He'd been taken there at gun point. Even on a hot summer's day with sweat beading his brow, Paladin mused, there would be no flies on the Bay City marshal.

Grey wanted to talk. He'd made sure Paladin was under lock and key before he got down to business.

Now he was leaning back against the wall opposite the cell, bathed in the warm light from the office's oil lamp. Coming at him from the side the light accentuated the angular planes of his face, left the sharp eyes in shadow.

'Despite the highfalutin name, this is a small town, Paladin. Not much goes unnoticed. So I know you rode in hot and dusty, accompanied by a feller looked meaner than a rattlesnake with toothache.'

'His name's Jack Breaker.'

'Ah.' Grey smiled. 'Another bell's clanging – real slow, like it tolls for a funeral. The moniker Breaker's got tagged on to those given names suggests he's a back shooter – and that from a safe distance.' He shook his head. 'I'm not all that fond of greasers, but if you ride with a cowardly killer like Breaker I'm even more inclined to give credence to the story they told.'

'I've tracked them all the way from a small town in Louisiana. Why would I do that, then call in here to talk to you if I'm a killer carrying—'

'Jim.'

The name was snapped by a stocky man who had followed his shadow in from the office. A deputy's badge gleamed on his vest.

'There's trouble over at the Al's place. Ellie came over. You want me to go?'

'Trouble, you say?' Grey said absently. He leaned his head back against the wall. 'This is Dave Ames, my deputy, Paladin, and that's the hotel he's talking about. Seems like this'll go down as a red letter day in little ole Bay City. What kind of trouble, Dave?'

'Those two greasers and this feller's pard arguing hard enough to end in gun play.'

Grey sighed. 'We'll both go,' he said, and pushed himself away from the wall. 'Paladin, you stay where you are, spend some time thinking up a story I might get close to believing.'

Tall, raw-boned, he followed the deputy out. Their shadows went with them. The light from the office lamp fell in a pool on the floor outside the cell.

Paladin stood up, walked across to the cell door. He

poked his hand through the bars. Then he pursed his lips thoughtfully.

The big bunch of keys was hanging in the lock.

Grey and his deputy were striding out, crossing the street at an angle, dark figures in a town that at night was lit just enough to make objects visible without disturbing anyone's sleep. His eyes on the two lawmen, Paladin stepped out of the office. Keeping tight against the walls, he made his way along the plank walk. His gun-belt had been hanging on a wooden hook. It was back around his waist. He'd checked the shells in his six-gun. All correct, though he wouldn't have put it past Jim Grey to empty the weapon's cylinder.

Yet the contradiction was staring Paladin in the face: why would any marshal walk away leaving his prisoner in a cell and the keys in the lock?

He was still juggling likely answers when the night's comfortable silence was rent apart by a burst of shooting from the direction of the hotel. The second floor front window's glass was lit by brilliant flashes in the room. Someone yelled, a blood-curdling roar that died away to a gurgle. There was another shot, and the window shattered, glass tinkling down on to the gallery's paper-thin roof.

The two lawmen had broken into a run when the first shots rang out. They bore down on the hotel, drawing their six-guns. As the window shattered, their boots were hammering on the three rickety steps leading on to the gallery. Both men ducked their heads as glass rained down, glittering shards falling on them through gaping holes in the roof. The stocky deputy, Dave Ames, had pulled ahead of Jim Grey. He made straight for the hotel's open front door and charged into the dark interior.

Paladin, still on the other side of the street, hugged the shadows and kept his eyes on the upstairs window. He'd drawn his six-gun. As yet there was no sign of movement. Just the shots, the loud roar that could have been anger, fear, or pain. Paladin needed a target, but was prepared to wait. The dangerous life he had led as a bounty hunter had left him with infinite patience.

Before Grey could reach the front door, there was another shot. Again Paladin saw the upstairs room brightly lit by a muzzle flash. Then, explosively, a man fell backwards through the shattered window. He took the frame with him. It was a short drop to the gallery roof. He hit it with his shoulders and neck. Under his weight the wood splintered with a crackling like the breaking of thin ice on a cold winter lake. Then he hit the board floor with a sickening crunch. Still caught in remnants of the wooden frame, he twitched, moaned, then lay still.

Jim Grey had spun as the man fell through the window, instinctively jumping away with his arms raised defensively as he crashed through the roof. Now he stepped close to him and dropped on one knee. With an effort he rolled him over, disentangled him from the frame.

Then he stood up and looked straight across the street at Paladin.

'The older Mexican,' he called. 'Broken neck – but he was dead before he fell, ugly knife wound in—'

A rattle of gunfire from the inside the hotel snapped his head around. He spun, brought his six-gun level as a man appeared out of the shadows. But he was walking backwards – and not doing it well. His stocky body was too slack, his legs wobbling. He reached the single step down, and it was his undoing. One boot touched the gallery's boards, but the leg could no longer take the man's weight. It collapsed under him. As he began to fall, Jim Grey sprang forward. He thrust both hands under the man's arms. For a second he tried to hold him. Then he too stumbled backwards and went down. Both men crumpled to the boards, Grey underneath. As they fell, the six-gun inside the hotel opened up again. Bullets whistled through the space where, seconds earlier, the two defence-less men had been standing.

Paladin had set off in a weaving run across the street before Jim Grey had finished calling to him. He was approaching the hotel when the two men fell, mounting the three steps while Grey was wriggling free of the dead weight. The bullets meant for Grey forced Paladin to throw himself desperately sideways. He rolled, came up as Grey was climbing to his feet. When the marshal looked across at Paladin, his face was grim.

'Dave Ames, my deputy,' he said. 'A fine man cut down—'

'Look out,' Paladin snapped, then again he leaped to one side as yet more shots sprayed the gallery.

Grey had also flung himself out of the line of fire. Now, for the first time he began to use his six-gun. He snapped a couple of fast shots into the shadowy passageway. Then, with a solid boom, the big heavy door slammed shut. Grey's next shot splintered the dark wood. There was a soft laugh from inside the hotel, then the sound of a bolt being driven home hard.

Without hesitation, Paladin made for the nearest down-stairs window. He used the butt of his six-gun to shatter the glass and clear jagged fragments from the frame. Then he threw a leg over the sill and dropped into the dark room.

Too much furniture, ill lit by light from the street. The smell of dust and mildew, unwashed bedding, stale sweat and cigarette smoke. The strong reek of cordite seeping in from the passageway.

The light from the street was barely strong enough to reach the room's closed door. Paladin could make out its panels, faintly gleaming. He blundered his way towards it, cursing out loud as he barked his shins on a low stool, then clamping his teeth shut to prevent the same mistake.

When he reached the door he pressed his ear to it; held his breath; listened. There was no sound in the passage-way. Behind him, on the other side of the shattered window, the gallery was silent. Grey was either waiting for the front door to be opened, or had run down the steps and into the alley leading to the rear of the building. That would make sense. The gunman had emptied his six-gun to keep heads down, then bolted the door. If he was going to make his escape, he'd do it by the back way.

Paladin stepped back from the door. As he did so, something wet dripped on to his face. Wet, and warm. He touched it with his finger; turned to what little light there was in the room. It was blood. He looked up. The ceiling was nothing more than the bare boards of the next floor. Through the cracks, dark blood oozed.

The room Paladin had booked with Breaker was directly overhead. The elder Rodriguez was lying dead on the gallery. Guillermo Rodriguez – it had to be him – had shot Dave Ames and then bolted the door. He was out there, somewhere. Putting two and two together it wasn't difficult to put a name to the man lying upstairs bleeding to death.

A voice called out from the street. There was a quiver in it, and Paladin knew the rattle of gunfire had disturbed someone's sleep. Then, as he stood listening, he heard a woman's voice. Her words were indistinguishable, but she was obviously distressed. Then she cried out, and Paladin heard a door at the rear of the hotel slam hard enough to shake rafters. It was followed seconds later by the rattle of horses' hoofs, rapidly fading into the distance.

In the seconds it took for that unseen drama to unfold, Paladin had been struggling with the door. Desperate to get out of the room, to help the woman, he had tugged at a door warped and swollen by damp. Abruptly it came free of the jamb, throwing him off balance. Then, with the sound of the back door's slamming a haunting echo in his ears, knowing he was far too late, he walked out into darkness. A left turn took him to the front door. He drew the bolt, pulled the door open.

The gallery was empty but for the body of Dave Ames. An old man was walking slowly across the street. A woman was watching from the far plankwalk.

'Go home, both of you,' Paladin called, 'it's all over.'

Then, pulling the wide door open to give himself some light, he went back down the passageway. There was a small reception area, a low counter. The register Paladin had signed lay open, a brass bell gleamed. In the faint light from the front door the blood glistened like wet paint on the bald head of the man lying on the worn carpet. He was breathing in ragged snorts, but strong enough to suggest to Paladin that he'd been knocked cold with the butt of a six-gun.

Then the back door banged open. Jim Grey stomped in.

'Gone,' he said. 'I got around there too late. He must have had a horse waiting, he was out of sight before—'

He broke off as he saw the man on the floor.

'Al Benson,' he said. 'Is he dead?'

'Out cold.'

'According to Dave it was Ellie reported this. His daughter. Where the hell's she got to?'

And there was a strained silence as he stared at Paladin with a distant look in his eyes. Paladin looked away, thought about what he'd heard and what it told him, knew that knowledge would keep.

'Someone's upstairs, bleeding through the ceiling,' he said, and headed for the stairs.

FOURTEEN

Jim Grey had walked the few yards down to the livery barn, found Curly Johnson looking phlegmatically up the street and told him what was needed. The hostler moved swiftly. When Paladin came down the stairs a buckboard had pulled up alongside the hotel's gallery and Grey and the hostler were struggling down the steps with the body of Dave Ames.

The hotel's owner had recovered consciousness. He was up on his feet, sagging against the counter. His face was sickly, his eyes unfocused.

Best they stay that way for a while, Paladin thought, and he walked outside.

'Another body upstairs,' he told Grey. 'Jack Breaker. Shot several times in the guts. It was him doing all the bleeding.'

Grey turned from the buckboard, hands on hips, catching his breath.

'So it was the Mexican kid I heard riding away?'

'Not just the kid.'

'Go on.'

116

'I was a while getting out of that front room. From what I could hear, he's got a woman with him.'

'That'll be Ellie Benson,' Grey said, and he banged his fist on the buckboard in sudden fury. 'If you knew that,' he said, glaring at Paladin, 'you must have been close, and if you were close, why the hell—?'

'You're wasting time. They're gone. If we're to catch them—'

'Come down to the jail,' Grey snapped. 'Curly, there's another body upstairs and I reckon Al needs the doc.'

And leaving the hostler looking up at the shattered upstairs window he strode briskly across the street.

'Guillermo Rodriguez must have had this planned from the start,' Paladin said. 'Breaker being in the same hotel made it easy for him. Him and his brother, they must have burst into Breaker's room. Breaker would have reacted, maybe got a couple of wild shots off, but reality is he was caught cold. One of the brothers – at a guess I'd say it was Alvaro – didn't risk going for a head shot but played safe and punched bullet holes in Breaker's middle. An ugly way to die.' He shook his head. 'And you say Alvaro was knifed?'

'Broke his neck in the fall, but he was bleeding from a knife wound.'

'Then I reckon the kid had come in behind his brother. Alvaro, a flashy Mexican, was probably preening himself on the way he'd downed Breaker. Then he sensed something was wrong, turned, got one shot off. Too wild, too late. Guillermo knifed him in the gut, then pushed him through the window. I told you about the leather case stuffed with money. That'll have gone with Guillermo.'

'That, and Ellie Benson,' Grey said.

'And that's the only bit I don't understand. Couldn't have been planned, had to be spur of the moment. A hostage must have seemed like a good idea, but it could be a fatal mistake.'

Grey nodded. 'Taking Ellie means the hunt won't give up till that kid's hanging from a tall tree.'

'His youthful looks are misleading. I keep calling him kid,' Paladin said, 'but according to Breaker he's pushing thirty. We should remember that, and take care.'

Grey had left the roll-top desk and was by the stove pouring coffee. With his back to Paladin he said, 'If I'm any judge of character, I'd say you've been taking too much care for too damn long.'

'Is that why you left the keys in the lock?'

Grey handed him his coffee, sat down.

'You heard Dave say there was trouble over at the hotel. I had no real reason to keep you locked up, and I wanted to see which way you'd run. You surprised me by not lighting out for distant parts, but confirmed what was just a hunch by doing damn all when the bullets started flying.'

'That hunch being?'

'You were a bounty hunter. Says a lot about the kind of man you were, but I guess it wore you out. All you can do now when there's trouble is stand well back and watch and dream about what used to be.'

'Harsh words, Grey.'

'And maybe I'll live to eat them,' Jim Grey said. 'I'm a pretty good town marshal, but I don't kid myself. Most men with nerve and commonsense and a liking for a boring daily routine in a quiet town could do my job. You have' – he grinned wryly – '*had* skills it'd take me a lifetime to acquire. You're a worn out bounty hunter too fond of strong drink, Paladin – that's another hunch – but I'm relying on you to stay sober long enough to hunt down this Mexican killer. And, while we're into the business of hunches, I reckon you'll do it for reasons you haven't yet mentioned.'

'Oh, there's more to my story than a couple of Mexes stealing a bagful of cash. This Guillermo kills for the fun of it, but this time he's—'

Grey's chair hit the desk with a bang as he sprang to his feet. Paladin swung round, his hand dropping to his gun.

'Ellie,' Jim Grey said softly, 'you just about stopped my heart walkin' in here like that. Where in the world have you been, girl?'

She was a pretty young woman with loose dark-hair, her plain clothing mostly hidden by a flowered smock. She took the cup of coffee Grey offered her, and sat down in his swivel chair smiling her thanks.

'I thought you knew,' she said. 'Dad told me there was trouble, so I called in here to warn you before taking the short walk to Mary Illingworth's home.

Grey rolled his eyes, spread his hands. 'I'm getting forgetful in my old age. Isn't Mary's first child due round about now?'

'A couple of days overdue,' Ellie said, pulling a face, 'which is why I was over there so late at night, and wearing a smock over my clothes.'

Grey nodded, but his thoughts were already moving on.

119

His face turned grave, and he shook his head. 'That trouble your dad mentioned got out of hand, Ellie. Dave Ames is dead. A couple more bodies have been taken away by Curly, and your dad got a nasty bang on the head.'

The young woman's eyes widened. 'Oh my goodness. Is Pa all right?'

'He'll have a headache for a while, but the doc reckons he'll be fine. You'll probably find him snoring in his bed.'

'But what was all that about when I walked in here?' Ellie said, both hands clasping her cup. 'You looked as if you'd seen a ghost, Jim.'

Grey flashed a glance at Paladin. 'The man doing most of the killing over at your place is a Mexican. When all the shooting was done he locked your front door, got away out the back. He moved fast. I was too late to catch him, or even set eyes on him. But before he left the hotel Paladin here thought he heard a woman talking, maybe crying out.'

'And you thought that was me? That this Mexican had taken me with him?'

'That seemed likely, but I guess Paladin was wrong.'

'No.' Paladin was emphatic. 'I know what I heard, Grey.'

'What you heard must have been the other woman,' Ellie said. 'She was by the counter talking to my dad when I came over here.'

Paladin spun on his heel, walked to the window, stood looking out at the street. His gaze was unseeing. He was remembering La Belle Commune and the look in Brad Corrigan's eyes, the message that was there to be read – and which Paladin had read, and misunderstood. And he was remembering his later dark foreboding, the frequent looks over his shoulder every time the back of his neck began to itch.

'All the way from Louisiana,' he said, 'I had a feeling we were being followed.'

There was a heavy silence behind him. It was broken by Grey.

'Are you saying it was this woman?'

'That's not possible,' Ellie said. 'She was old, fragile, a thin stick of a woman.'

Paladin swung around. 'There was a lot of dirty, night-time fighting back in La Belle Commune. Emma Bowman-Laing was prowling around in the woods watching most of it, ready to ride in and pick up the pieces. The town marshal, Brad Corrigan, was one of those pieces; he's alive because of her.' Paladin laughed harshly. 'Hell, after the courage she showed a little old ride of a couple of hundred miles wouldn't faze her.'

'Whether it did or it didn't,' Grey said quietly, 'if you've got it right she's now in the hands of a Mexican killer. Nothing's changed except the name of the woman, Paladin.'

Ellie had turned a little pale, perhaps thinking of what might have been if she had lingered in the hotel just a few minutes longer. She put down her cup and rose to her feet. 'Thanks for the drink, Jim. I'll go and see Pa and leave you two to sort this out. I hope you do. I feel so sorry for that poor old woman.'

'But you don't, do you?' Grey said to Paladin as the door closed behind the young woman.

'Mixed feelings. I've known her a while now, and

common sense tells me she's in danger. But she's a tough old bird, and I'm wondering what went on between her and that Mexican. Has she been taken against her will? Or did she come up with some story that persuaded him to take her along?'

'Why the hell would she do that?'

'For the same reason she followed me and Breaker. She knew Breaker was behind most of the killing in La Belle Commune, but it was bullets from Rodriguez's six-gun that did all the damage. I told her the Rodriguez brothers had double-crossed him – the kid had told Breaker a phoney story from the start – but it made no difference: far as Bowman-Laing was concerned, Breaker was a no-good outlaw and could never be trusted. As for me, she watched me in action and wasn't impressed.'

'Well I'll be a monkey's uncle,' Grey said softly. Knowing shrewdly what Paladin was suggesting, there was a frown of utter disbelief furrowing his brow.

'You and me both,' Paladin said. 'There were two Mexicans when we started out on the trail. Now there's just the one. Bowman-Laing saw the way the wind was blowing, and seized her chance. I think there's a real possibility she intends taking him all on her own.'

FIFTEEN

'Rodriguez, I think we should stop and bed down for what's left of the night,' Emma Bowman-Laing called.

They had ridden due north out of Bay City, putting the gulf coast behind them and heading at breakneck speed into a flat, moonlit landscape of tangled scrub and parched trees with gnarled trunks. It seemed to Bowman-Laing that the Mexican must know that part of Texas, for he rode steadily and without hesitation across rough terrain without landmarks or any point of reference. She quickly came to the realization that the ability to find their way unerringly in a strange land was a skill honed to perfection in Rodriguez and his fellow outlaws. All too often they were fleeing from pursuing posses, running into an impenetrable wilderness in a desperate attempt to save their lives.

After she called to him she drew rein close to one of the trees, her gloved hand absently stroking the chestnut mare's wet neck. She knew Rodriguez had heard her, though he rode on for several hundred yards. As she waited patiently for his return, she sat relaxed in the saddle and let her thoughts wander.

She had always stayed well behind Paladin and Breaker on the ride from Louisiana. When she rode into a Bay City lit only by lamplight she had heard the fierce bursts of gunfire. Intuition had told her that Breaker must be involved. Quickly pin-pointing the sounds she had ridden her mare around the back of the hotel. Another horse was tethered there. When she dismounted and went into the building through the back door, the first thing that drew her gaze in the dim light was the body of a man lying on the floor by the counter. Her heart began thumping. Her mouth went dry.

Then Rodriguez came bounding down the stairs. He had a smoking six-gun in one hand. In the other he was carrying a heavy leather bag. In his excitement he was almost dancing across the passage, stepping lightly on the balls of his feet. He saw Bowman-Laing, recognized her at once and lifted his six-gun. She saw the killing light glinting in his black eyes, his white teeth bared in a ferocious grin, and quickly thrust out a hand as if to ward off the bullet.

'Goodness me, don't do that, Rodriguez,' she'd said, 'you need me with you.' And, as quickly as an old woman could, she turned and ran for the back door.

She had spoken in haste, the words tumbling out in a desperate attempt to save her life. It was likely that when he considered himself reasonably safe from immediate pursuit he would realize his mistake in allowing her to ride with him. When that moment came, she was finished. On the frantic flight from town she had been riding with the ease of one who had learned to ride as a child, all the while racking her brain for some way of convincing the outlaw that he did need her and should let the old lady live.

She had been able to come up with just the one reason, and it was a possibility only, founded on her belief in man's goodness: she was an old lady far from home, and needed his help. But this man was an outlaw, a wicked man. If that failed – as she knew damn well it would – she needed another reason that would appeal to his darker side. Her only hope was that if she could keep him talking something would emerge.

And now Rodriguez had slowed his horse, turned, and was coming back to her. She watched his approach, put a good deal of feigned weariness into her smile.

'I'm exhausted. They won't come after you tonight. They might not come after you at all.'

'It was a deputy marshal I shot,' Guillermo Rodriguez said. He had dismounted, and was taking the opportunity to take the banknotes from the leather bag and stuff them into his saddle-bags. 'They will hunt me down relentlessly and hang me from the nearest tree. You have blankets. I will leave you here.' He grinned. 'It would not be wise to stay with you and perhaps fall asleep. I do not fully understand why you are with me in the first place, but think perhaps you intend to kill me.'

Oh yes, Bowman-Laing thought, *oh yes, Señor Rodriguez, that's exactly what I intend to do. Perhaps not here, and not by my own hand, but there is another who can do it much better than I.*

She raised her eyebrows. 'Really? You think I'm after all that money?'

He shrugged, sent the empty leather case crashing into

the scrub and buckled the saddle-bags. 'That would naturally be yours once I am dead. But I think you mostly wish to avenge the deaths of those men in La Belle Commune.'

'If you think that, why did you agree to let me ride with you?'

'In the hotel there was much danger and I was careful of my life so in too much of a hurry to protest.'

'I want you to take me home,' Bowman-Laing said. 'You owe me that much.'

'I owe you nothing.'

'Wasn't it you put a flaming torch to my house and burned it to the ground?'

'Is unimportant. The house was old, of no use.'

'It was where I was born.' She looked at him, thought of his background, how village Mexicans would have strong family ties, and presented him with her first attempt to convince him.

'You can pretend I'm your mother,' she said.

'My mother was many years ago shot dead.'

'That's awful. I'm so sorry.'

'Again, is unimportant.' His smile was cruel. 'The man who was responsible is now also dead. In Bay City there was at last some recompense.'

Bowman-Laing was frowning. 'Bay City? Then you must mean Jack Breaker.'

'When it happened I was very young, but I have always a good memory.' He nodded. 'Breaker, yes, he was there and he is dead so now it is finished.'

'Then take me home, Guillermo,' she said softly, and using her knuckles to press her lips against her teeth and cause pain she looked at him with eyes in which bright

126

tears welled. But behind that façade, her thoughts were racing.

Guillermo Rodriguez had presented her with the key.

'*Es ridiculoso,*' he said, 'and you are a most stupid woman. I leave you now, before it is too late and I am caught.'

'You were wrong about Breaker.'

He frowned. 'I remember well. Breaker, and the other men from Texas, their horses still wet from crossing the Bravo.'

'Oh, Jack Breaker was there all right, and I'm sure he was using his six-gun. But the bullet that killed your mother was not fired by Breaker.'

'Who then? You know?'

'In La Belle Commune, quite recently, there was a very sick man,' Bowman-Laing said. 'The town's doctor can't be trusted, so I took this sick man back to my lodge in the woods close to my old house where I nursed him back to life.' She smiled sadly. 'He was delirious. In his rambling he talked about you, how he had recognized you when you rode through the town. He is the man who shot your mother, Rodriguez, and he's well known in La Belle Commune. His name is Brad Corrigan.'

SIXTEEN

Paladin and Grey set off after Guillermo Rodriguez as the first rays of the sun were brightening the eastern horizon and touching the high false fronts of Bay City's buildings. Better that way, Grey had insisted. A couple of hours start was nothing, so why follow an outlaw in the dark when he could leave the trail and kill them both from ambush.

So in the heavy silence that settled over the town after the shooting they had snatched what rest they could, and Paladin had revised his thinking. As they prepared to leave he suggested to Grey that rather than killing Rodriguez – which, if Emma had played on the image of an old woman then taken him by surprise, could have been done without leaving the hotel – she intended slowing him down by whatever means she could cook up.

Grey was unimpressed and deliberately refused to speculate. The whole idea of an old woman riding all the way from Louisiana then hanging on to an outlaw's coat tails was too difficult to swallow.

They collected their horses from Curly Johnson's barn, thrust Winchester repeating rifles into leather saddle boots, then moved off up the street. There was only one way Rodriguez could have left town from his starting point, Grey said. He led Paladin down the alleyway alongside the side of the hotel, checked the ground and saw the unmistakable signs of the outlaw's hurried departure, then struck out across the barren outskirts of Bay City before turning to head north.

Once clear of the town they rode hard and fast for thirty minutes. There was a trail but it was now little used, the deep ruts overgrown with grass and weeds. In a swift aside, not taking his eyes off the way ahead, Grey told Paladin the trail's condition helped in tracking Rodriguez. Paladin agreed. Even he could see the fresh imprints of horses' hoofs, the torn or flattened grass, the occasional droppings.

When they had covered ten miles, Grey abruptly sat straight in the saddle and slowed the pace to a walk. Paladin pulled alongside. Grey nodded to the right. His face was grim, his voice harsh.

'You see what I see?'

The landscape was little changed: gently undulating, covered in rough scrub for as far as the eye could see. It was a ragged stand of grey-green, withered cottonwoods that Grey was indicating. The rising sun was casting long shadows, but no shadow could hide the shocking sight that met their eyes.

'That's Emma Bowman-Laing,' Paladin said hoarsely, and he spurred his horse off the trail.

Rodriguez had tied the old lady to the gnarled trunk of one of the cottonwood trees and left her to die.

Paladin got to her first. He kicked his feet free of the

stirrups and hit the ground running. He rushed to the tree, rested one hand high on the trunk's rough bark as he leaned close. Bowman-Laing's thin body was sagging, supported painfully by the binding ropes. Rodriguez had made damn sure she couldn't move. A rope bound her ankles to the tree, another encircled her slender waist, a third was high up under her armpits. Her head had fallen forward so that her chin was on her chest. Her thick grey hair was hiding her face.

'Emma?' Paladin said softly, and he reached out with great tenderness and lifted her chin.

'She's alive,' Grey said.

Paladin cupped her chin and held the weight of her head in the palm of his hand. Deeply sunken blue eyes looked at him through lids narrowed to slits. Unbelievably, thin lips puckered by lines of pain and old age twitched in an attempt at a smile.

'Knew you'd come, Paladin,' she mumbled – and then she fainted.

The fire sent a thin plume of white smoke into brilliant blue skies. Severed ropes lay like dead snakes around the base of the cottonwood tree. Close enough to the fire to warm her old, abused bones, Emma Bowman-Laing lay with her head on Jim Grey's saddle. One of his blankets covered her from her shoulders to her toes.

Suspended from a curved branch poked into the ground, a coffee pot bubbled over the flames, tended to by Jim Grey. Paladin had just asked Bowman-Laing what had happened. She answered with a despairing shake of the head followed by a rush of words.

'I told that Mexican that Brad was one of a bunch of wild Texans led by Jack Breaker,' she said, 'and that it was Brad who killed his mother. It was a crazy, wicked lie, but I knew it would be enough to send him hot-foot back to La Belle Commune. I was banking on him taking me with him; I'd already asked him to take me home. Of course, I was going by the response I would expect from a good man, but this man is wicked. He spoke not another word. Tied me to the tree. Took my horse, headed east for the border at a fair old lick.'

Jim Grey poured coffee into tin cups. Bowman-Laing lifted herself on to one elbow. Paladin handed her a drink, steadying her hand with his as she lifted the cup shakily to her lips.

'Putting two and two together,' Paladin said, 'I suppose Rodriguez killed Breaker for the same reason that's taken him after Brad.'

'Of course. He thought it was Breaker who had shot his mother. And now, thanks to my stupidity, he's going to kill poor old Brad, unless you can get to him first – and that's going to be tough because he's got two horses and a couple of hours' start on you.'

'Leave now,' Jim Grey said, and he winked at Paladin. 'As soon as this brave young lady's strong enough, I'll throw her across my saddle and take her back to Bay City.'

'Foolhardy, not brave,' Bowman-Laing said bitterly. 'And I deserve being thrown somewhere. What in the world was I thinking of, horning in on men's work?'

Paladin stroked her hand before rising to his feet and walking away. 'Your heart was in the right place,' he said, pausing for a moment, 'and, strange though it may seem, it's worked out for the best. For one thing, you've saved me from a manhunt clear across Texas to the Rio Grande. And though Brad's unlikely to be expecting trouble back there in La Belle Commune, he's a tough old bird with sharp eyes and doesn't miss much.'

'Tough, but getting old, Paladin,' she called to his back.

'Yeah, well, I don't know about you,' Paladin said as he reached his horse and swung into the saddle, 'but I can't imagine a better lookout post for an old man than that rocking chair of his creaking out there in the afternoon sun.'

SEVENTEEN

It had taken Paladin and Breaker a week to reach Bay City after crossing the Sabine River. By riding night and day, cat-napping when he could, Paladin retraced his steps to the banks of the big river in three days. It was a cool dawn, the wide waters glinting in the early sunlight. He and Breaker had crossed further upstream where they had found a stony ford. Here he would be forced to swim his horse across. The water was calm, with little current, but one look at the exhausted animal flecked with white foam told Paladin swimming wasn't possible for either of them without a few hours' sleep.

He cursed softly, then shook his head at his foolish impatience and took the horse down the grassy bank to a patch of wet gravel. He allowed it to lap up just enough of the cold water to slake its thirst, then pulled it away. He looked around. There was a stand of trees fifty yards down-stream. They would find shade there as the sun climbed higher in the skies and the temperature soared. By after-noon they'd both be rested. La Belle Commune was another two days' ride, but Paladin knew he must be closing in on Rodriguez. The Mexican might have a strong spare mount, but even using two horses a man can ride only so fast.

He was halfway to the trees when the bullet ripped across his left shoulder, sending a lightning bolt of agony clear to his fingertips. The blow was powerful enough to throw him sideways against the startled horse. In the same instant he heard the flat crack of the rifle from across the water. His numbed left hand slipped from the reins. Knowing instinctively where Rodriguez would plant his next shot he punched the horse's rump with a clenched fist, sucked in a breath and screamed a wild rebel yell. The horse whinnied shrilly in protest, settled back on its haunches then bolted.

Paladin went down. He hit the dry ground hard with his wounded shoulder. Pain was liquid fire coursing through muscle and bone. For an instant he blacked out.

Consciousness returned to the crack of the distant rifle and the sound of a bullet thudding into the earth close to his head. His shirt was already soaked with blood, his head singing. Clenching his teeth, knowing what he must do because there was no other way to save himself, he waited tensely for the next bullet. When it buried itself in the ground within inches of his hip Paladin let go a scream of agony and flung up an arm. Then he rolled on to his back and lay still.

In the sudden silence he could hear his pulse hammering, the gentle lapping of the river on the gravel beneath the bank; the hiss of his breath through clenched teeth as he tried to blank out the pain and steel himself for death.

Then, from across the water, the sound of hoofs. Two

horses, unhurried, but moving steadily away into the distance.

Paladin turned over, pressed his face against the cool grass, closed his eyes and slowed his breathing. When he opened his eyes again the sun was high in the sky, its hot rays burning his back. He groaned and moved, but much too jerkily. He reached out to push himself up on to his knees. The movement tore his shirt from the drying blood on his shoulder with a dry ripping sound.

The pain was excruciating.

Once again Paladin blacked out.

EIGHTEEN

Two days later Brad Corrigan was lazily soaking up the late afternoon sun. His eyes were closed. He and Shorty Long were taking it easy, nursing healing wounds and muscles stiff from digging graves for the bodies of dead outlaws. The rocking-chair in front of La Belle Commune's jail creaked soporifically to the easy pushing of Corrigan's right foot. He was dozing, half listening to the rhythmic creaking, the distant sounds of the sea lapping the shore beyond Salty's Notch, an off-key honky-tonk piano.

The marshal smiled without opening his eyes. Shorty Long had taken over the running of Paulson's saloon, and he was tinkling the yellowing ivories. But he was still the town's hostler. There was a jangling cacophony. The music stopped, a lid banged down and minutes later Corrigan heard the uneven stamp of boots on the gallery across the street as Long left the saloon.

Off to his stables, Corrigan thought, and he yawned and opened his eyes. As he did so he became aware of the muffled thud of a horse's hoofs in the dust. At the same time, Shorty Long, halfway across the street, pulled up. He was squinting into the western sun.

'Brad,' he called warningly.

'I hear,' Corrigan said, cocking his head. 'Trotting, but not too easy. Who is it?'

Long walked down the middle of the street. Corrigan was up on his feet. He tipped his Derby hat over his eyes, looked into the setting sun.

'Dammit,' he said softly as Long moved to intercept the horse, 'that's Bowman-Laing's chestnut mare.'

The mare saw Long in front of her, lifted her head and began to turn away. But she was flecked with foam, her eyes showing the whites as she kept her head lifted and turned to one side so that the trailing reins were clear of her forelegs. Long stepped close, grabbed the reins close to the bit. Uttering soothing words, he leaned his weight back to pull her to a halt and ran his hand up and down her wet neck. The horse stopped. Her legs were trembling, nostrils flared as she fought for breath.

Long was looking at the saddle. Then he bent, lightly touched the open, bloody gashes on her body, and he uttered a soft curse.

'Some sonofabitch,' he said, 'has been riding this mare hard, raking her with spurs. She's bleeding, plumb wore out, been ridden to a standstill.'

He turned angrily, began to lead the horse away.

'Why'd you look at the saddle?'

'If the rider was shot, there might have been blood,' Long said. 'I didn't see any.'

'Dammit, the rider was Emma,' Corrigan said fiercely. He was walking with the hostler, his clenched hands showing white knuckles as he looked behind him, to the side, searching aimlessly. 'She rode out after Paladin and Breaker with no clear idea of what she was about. I warned her, tried to stop her. . . .' He shook his head. 'Something must've gone badly wrong, but how far did she get? What happened to her, and where?'

'She's a feisty lady, but Paladin and Breaker were chasing those two Mexicans,' Long said. He looked grimly at Corrigan. 'That young Mexican is a cold-blooded killer. By the look of this horse, the feller riding her was using spurs with big Mexican rowels.'

His message was clear. Corrigan felt hollow. He stopped, stood with hands on hips. His eyes searched the street, the rough ground between the wide-spaced shacks where late afternoon shadows fell; the grassy slopes leading up to the Bowman-Laing bridge over Petit Creek and beyond that the shell of the old house.

'If you're right, and it's the young Mexican, why has he come back – and then that same question: where the hell is he now?'

'I don't know.' Shorty Long had stopped with him. He was holding the exhausted mare still, gentling her with his hand as he watched Corrigan with concern. 'I tend horses, Brad, spend time in the saloon playing the piano when I'm not serving drinks. You, you're a tough old cattle-town marshal—'

'All right, I'll give you my opinion,' Corrigan snapped. 'Yes, it's the young Mexican. That's a hunch, and when they're mine, I trust them. The way I'm picturing it, he's been using two horses and he came back here in one hell of a hurry. On the edge of town he let Emma's mare go, then went his way.' His face was bleak. There was pain naked in his eyes. 'I don't know where Bowman-Laing is, I don't know why the Mex has come back, but this is a clear warning, Shorty: *look what I've done*, he's sayin', *now make a guess on what I'll do next*. And I wouldn't be one bit surprised if at this very moment that Mexican kid isn't out there, swigging out of a jar of mescal while he watches us over the sights of a rifle.'

To Paladin, it seemed like the longest ride of his life. The way he felt it had taken a whole year, with those 365 days squeezed into two that from dawn to dusk were exquisite agony.

When he saw some way ahead of him the shacks of La Belle Commune shimmering in the heat haze, he was a dried-out shell parched by the overhead sun and clinging to the saddle horn with what remained of his strength. On the banks of the wide river he had bandaged the wound in his shoulder with the sleeves torn from his shirt. In the two days it had taken him to get from the Sabine to La Belle Commune, his shoulder had not for one minute stopped throbbing.

Yet, plumb tuckered-out, famished, dry as the proverbial bone and as weak as a day old kitten, Paladin was clear-headed. Not once during that ride had he failed to keep his eyes skinned for any sign of Guillermo Rodriguez. Not once had he ridden through a stand of trees or taken his horse under the shadow of a tree-lined bluff without constantly scanning the slopes and ridges for the ideal site for a bushwhack.

There had been no sign of the man. No crack of a rifle, no bullet piercing his flesh to add to his pain. Paladin had made it all the way to La Belle Commune with just the one painful fall from his horse when he sank into a deep sleep in the saddle – but what about Brad Corrigan? If there had been no sign of Rodriguez on the trail, the Mexican had swallowed Paladin's theatrical dying act, dismissed the once-feared bounty hunter from his mind and concentrated on what lay ahead. What spurred the Mexican on was the story he had been fed of a devil in human clothing: Brad Corrigan, the renegade Texan Bowman-Laing had told him had killed his mother.

And the town, as Paladin rode in, was ominously quiet.

The honky-tonk piano jangled discordantly as Shorty Long's hands banged down on the yellow ivories. He froze in that position, leaning half forward with his hand spread wide. He could feel the tender skin around his healing bullet wound stretching painfully as his eyes stared at the intricate gold design on the old piano's panels close to his nose.

The ring of the six-gun's muzzle pushed warm and hard against the nape of his neck. Long's mouth went dry at the sound of the weapon cocking.

'If you are Brad Corrigan,' a soft voice said, 'you should perhaps remember your childhood prayers while you have time.'

'I'm not Corrigan.'

'No. You are too small, too insignificant. Is clear to me that I have the wrong man. But you know where he is, of course.'

'Take that damned gun away from my neck, Rodriguez.'

There was a wicked chuckle. The muzzle was removed.

Booted feet scraped. Long turned cautiously on the rickety stool. Rodriguez had stepped back. Silhouetted by the backdrop of bright sunlight in the saloon's open doorway he was a figure larger than life, his tasselled sombrero casting a grotesque shadow. The light flooding through the doorway glinted on the silver conchos decorating his hat band.

He waggled the shiny six-gun menacingly.

'Where is Brad Corrigan?'

'I don't know any Corrigan.'

'Is a pity, but *no es importante.* I am quite content to kill every man who gives me the wrong answer. When I get the right answer, I will kill Corrigan.'

'I don't know who this Corrigan is,' Long said, 'but killing me won't help you find him.'

'*Es verdadero.* So perhaps there is another way. If you are a man of some importance in this apology for a town and I take you outside into the sun with a gun at your throat—'

'What's going on here, Shorty?'

Like a startled lizard, Rodriguez took refuge. In a blur of movement he took several dancing steps that put him behind Long. He was much taller than the little hostler and so not entirely hidden, but the ring of the six-gun's muzzle was once again at the nape of Long's neck.

'Ah,' Rodriguez said softly as sunlight reflected from the mirror behind the bar touched Corrigan's face, glinted on his badge of office. 'Is a dead man, risen again. Next time I will be sure to shoot very straight.'

'He's looking for a feller called Corrigan,' Shorty Long said.

'What's he want with him?'

'Wants him dead.'

'Why?'

'Many years ago,' Rodriguez said, 'this Corrigan was with renegades who cross the Bravo with Jack Breaker. When they attack my *pueblo*, Corrigan, he shoot and kill my mother. I have killed Breaker. So now. . . .'

There was a sudden silence. Corrigan's face had hardened. Then he shrugged.

'Wish I could help,' he said, 'but being entirely truthful, I can't say I've ever come face to face with the man.'

Despite the deadly ring of steel, Long chuckled.

Rodriguez pushed him away, hard. Long's gammy leg gave beneath him. Deliberately, he emphasized the stumble. He fell against Corrigan, clutched at the marshal's clothing for support. When he straightened and stepped away, Corrigan had turned half sideways and his six-gun had vanished from its holster.

Rodriguez had not spotted the bold move. He shook his head impatiently. 'Is a very old woman I see in Bay City,' he said. 'She lives here, I have seen her, she is perhaps familiar to you. My actions in dealing with Breaker were impressive to her. So she told me this about Corrigan, this shooting of my mother. Also, she say he is well known in this town. If she is right, you are wrong. So I find out. Is easy. You tell me, or you die.'

'You'd better hold that questioning for a little while, rest your trigger finger,' Corrigan said. 'I hear a rider, and it sounds as if he's coming this way.'

Paladin rode warily. Once he was within the town limits, the electric tension that was crackling in the air drove all aches and pains to a hidden recess in his mind. He listened with straining ears, probed every possible hiding place with eyes that were never still; paid particular attention to the sixth sense that in the past had many times saved his life.

The wide street was deserted. A hot dry breeze sent a torn scrap of paper skittering in a cloud of dust. Paladin rode through it, eyes narrowed. He pushed on to the jail, and there he drew rein. His sixth sense was screaming a warning.

The afternoon sun was warm on his back, but the sight of the empty rocking chair sent a chill down his spine. Guillermo Rodriguez had come to La Belle Commune hunting Brad Corrigan. When Paladin turned his gaze across the street, he saw Rodriguez's horse tied outside Paulson's place.

'Well now,' he murmured. 'So this is where it ends.'

And he dismounted with difficulty, tied his horse and started across the street.

He walked stiffly, picking his steps with care because of the weakness that he knew was only in abeyance. He drew his six-gun. Without taking his eyes off Paulson's place he checked the cylinder's loads silently and by the touch of his fingers on the bullets' round noses, let it fall lightly back into the holster. In the soft dust of the street his booted feet moved with a whisper of sound, but his eyes looked with misgivings at the loose steps leading up on to the gallery: climbing those in silence would be an impossibility.

When he reached the hitch rail, he thoughtfully touched Rodriguez's horse, ran his hand down its neck as it nudged him with its head. He squinted up at the saloon's open door. If Rodriguez was in there, a man climbing those creaking steps would be alerting the Mexican gunman. Walking into that dim room with the sun at his back, he would be committing suicide. But if he circled the building and went in through the back door the situation would be reversed. His approach would be unexpected, and the sun's location would be in his favour.

Paladin slapped the horse's rump. It whinnied, stepped its rear end sideways, tail swishing; whinnied again in protest.

Now Rodriguez knows I'm here, out front, he thought with satisfaction.

Then as fast as stiff muscles and almost useless left arm would allow, Paladin ran for the side alleyway. The salt tang of the sea was cool on his face, but all too reminiscent of the scent and taste of freshly spilled blood.

NINETEEN

'I give you my opinion,' Guillermo Rodriguez said. 'It is Paladin out there. I kill him on the banks of the Sabine, but he is like the tall marshal here: he rise from the dead.'

'You're a lousy shot,' Corrigan said.

'That is a matter of opinion, and perhaps a big mistake.'

Out in front of the saloon a horse whinnied, then again. Rodriguez grinned savagely.

'Paladin was a bounty hunter,' Corrigan said. 'He downed your pal Flint without too much trouble and now he's coming after you.'

'Bounty hunters are insignificant. And you must understand that if this Paladin comes through that door with his six-gun blazing, one of you will be the first to die.' His teeth flashed. 'I will leave you in suspense.'

Then, behind him, a door banged open.

'Drop it, Rodriguez.'

Paladin had his six-gun out and cocked. He was defeated by the bewildering speed of the slim Mexican.

Without hesitation, Rodriguez shot Shorty Long in the throat. Then he sprang at Corrigan. The six-gun Long had been hiding clattered to the ground. The little hostler fell with a gurgling cry. He was behind the unarmed Corrigan. The marshal stumbled over his body as Rodriguez's shoulder slammed into his chest. His hat fell off and rolled under the tables. Then the Mexican was behind him. He whipped a sinewy arm around the marshal's throat and held him in a choking headlock. He poked his six-gun under Corrigan's arm and fired two shots towards Paladin. Then he began dragging Corrigan along the bar towards the door.

The shots drove Paladin back against the kitchen doorway as he ducked the hot lead. He had badly misjudged the opposition, and he'd been wrong about the light. Rodriguez and Corrigan were outlined against the bright rectangle of the open doorway, but the dazzling light in Paladin's eyes turned the room as dark as a cave. Rodriguez was clutching the marshal too close to him for Paladin to risk a shot. Halfway along the bar the Mexican flung the marshal bodily away from him, hooked a foot around his ankle. Corrigan hit the floor hard, roaring in frustration and pain. Exposed but now free to run, Rodriguez used the light and the shadows. One second he was visible to Paladin, the next he had dropped to the side and was lost. Paladin's eyes were adjusting. He had time for one swift shot that drew splinters close to the Mexican's head. Then it was too late. Rodriguez darted out of the shadows and into the light once more – then he was gone.

Paladin stepped further into the room and took a quick

look at Long. The hostler was lying motionless in a pool of blood.

'Shorty's dead,' Corrigan said over the rattle of receding hoofbeats. Up on his feet, the marshal was looking for his hat. He located it, kicked the table out of the way, slapped on the battered Derby and said, 'Get after that feller, Paladin. I'll go see Doc Foster, tell him to arrange a buckboard to collect Shorty's body. Then I'll grab me some weapons and shells from the jail and follow you on up.'

'On up where?'

Corrigan's grin was bleak. 'That Mex is after a man called Corrigan. He's not about to leave town, and my guess is he'll take to the high ground. He'll be making for the Bowman-Laing bridge.'

'It was Bowman-Laing who put him on to you.'

'Yeah, so he said. An old woman in Bay City. I find it hard to believe.'

'She told it to me herself when I cut her down from the tree.' Paladin flapped a hand at the marshal's wide-eyed consternation. 'She's unhurt, and had her reasons for what she did, but that's for later. We need to get Rodriguez before he gets you. I stopped by his horse out at the front rail. He's got a rifle and I was a fool not to take it. With that, in cover, he'll be difficult to shift.'

The sun was low. Once Paladin had pushed his horse across the long grassy slopes and was into the trees sheltering the upper reaches of Petit Creek, the shadows were long. The smell of the creek was rank, but almost overpowered by the lingering stench of smoke and charred wood from the ruined house.

Paladin had again been expecting Rodriguez to attempt an ambush from the cover of the timber, and so had ridden with care, his six-gun always at the ready. Against a rifle, from any decent range, that was about as much use as a slingshot against a charging grizzly. But there was no ambush. The woods were silent but for the rustle of leaves in the faint breeze, the crackle of twigs marking Paladin's progress. He took his horse across the bridge, the echo of its hoofs on the shaky timber sending roosting birds flapping and squawking from the undergrowth. When he reached the edge of the trees and drew rein to look across the ruined lawns fronting the big house, realization hit him with a jolt. Corrigan had said Rodriguez would make for the high ground. What the wily old marshal had been telling Paladin – without spelling it out – was that it was in Emma Bowman-Laing's old house that Guillermo Rodriguez would make his last stand.

And, by God, Paladin vowed, this would be his last.

The house was a blackened shell, but for a man with a rifle it was ideal cover. The fire had burnt upwards fiercely, but the unnatural downdraught that had come whirling through the trees had stopped it in its tracks. In any fire-gutted building, it's always the stairs that are left standing. Rodriguez would use those, find footing on what was left of the floors and position himself alongside a window. Rooting him out of there would be like trying to get a clam out of its shell.

Those thoughts were occupying one part of Paladin's mind when he heard the rattle of hoofs on timber behind him and knew Corrigan had reached the bridge. That split-second distraction was almost his undoing. The crack of the rifle was followed by a puff of smoke from a downstairs window. A green overhanging branch took the impact of the bullet, split, whipped Paladin across the face. He rocked sideways in the saddle, cursing, and a second bullet was an angry bee buzzing uncomfortably close to his right ear.

'Pop a few shots in his direction from time to time,' Corrigan called. 'I'll cut through the woods behind the house, leave my horse and take him from the rear.'

'There's fresh graves in there, Brad.'

'Well let's make damn sure the next one you dig is for that Mex.'

'It will be. When I hear you open fire, I'll come running.'

'Don't drag your heels. I'm a tired old man with a bullet hole in his back.'

Corrigan tossed over a box of shells which Paladin caught deftly, then brush crackled as the Derby-hatted marshal took his horse into the woods where Paulson and Mackie lay buried. Prudently out of the saddle and back under cover, Paladin tracked his progress by sound. He wondered if Rodriguez were doing the same, and thought it likely. But even if the Mexican knew he was being outflanked it didn't lessen the danger he faced.

To add to Rodriguez's problems and help Corrigan move in unobserved, Paladin slipped his Winchester from its boot and planted a couple of shots through the centre of the downstairs window. They whacked into the room's back wall with hollow thuds.

He was rewarded by merry laughter. An answering

volley came from an upstairs window. The bullets sliced through high branches. Leaves fluttered like moths around Paladin's head.

Then, in a show of bravado and brazen defiance, Guillermo Rodriguez stepped out on to the first-floor balcony. He lifted his rifle and waved it aloft, then swept off his colourful sombrero and executed an elaborate bow.

The defiant, theatrical pose ended abruptly. Corrigan must have chosen that moment to charge into the building from the rear. Rodriguez spun on his heel. Paladin tried another long shot and saw it chip fragments of blackened glass from the window frame. One must have hit Rodriguez as he fled, for he clapped a hand to his face. Then he was gone, inside the ruins. Shots rang out, muffled by distance and intervening walls.

Paladin slipped the rifle back into its boot. He hitched his horse's reins to a tree, took shells from the box and filled his belt loops. Then he set off at a loping run across the lawns to the house.

TWENTY

When Paladin slowly and cautiously slipped inside he entered a blackened wasteland. The stink of charred wood stung the nostrils. Boots crunched through wooden debris, tinkled through the broken glass of fallen, shattered chandeliers. The slightest movement kicked up fine grey ash. It settled on clothes, hands, face, coated the inside of nostrils.

The wide, once magnificent staircase lay ahead of him. Looking beyond that towards the back of the house Paladin saw the tall figure of Brad Corrigan. The marshal's six-gun was out. He'd fired the shots that had pulled a startled Rodriguez off the balcony, sent the signal to Paladin. Now he came crunching through the rubble towards the bounty hunter.

Paladin touched his lips with a finger, then pointed upwards. Corrigan shook his head.

'There's no sense in keeping quiet,' he shouted. 'That Mex killer knows we're here. He's going to sit tight up there, let us do the hard, dangerous work.'

Softly, Paladin said, 'You know this place. Any other stairs?'

'Sure,' Corrigan said, lowering his voice. 'At the back of the house. The servants used those.'

'So we split up.'

'Only way.'

'You go up the back stairs. Make plenty of noise.'

'And draw his fire?' Corrigan grinned. 'I can see why you survived for so long.'

'We time it so we reach the next floor together.'

'Yeah.' Corrigan nodded. For a second he looked pensively at Paladin. Then he took a couple of steps to the side. The stairway turned back on itself between each floor. Corrigan peered up the stair well.

'You hear me, Rodriguez?' he yelled.

'Of a certainty.' The voice was mocking.

'I'm the Brad Corrigan you're lookin' for. The tall feller wearing the badge; you had me in a stranglehold – remember? You're wrong about me: I've never been to Mexico in my life. But you murdered a couple of my friends, so you keep that gun ready because I'm coming up the back stairs.'

Then, with a wink at Paladin he walked over to the main staircase.

You crafty sonofabitch, Paladin thought, and grinned wryly. He watched as Corrigan reached the foot of the staircase, stopped and looked back. Paladin held up a hand: '*Wait there*,' he mouthed. Then he lifted his six-gun, raised one finger, and hoped the marshal understood that one shot would be the signal to start climbing.

Then Paladin ran for the rear of the house.

There, the much narrower back stairs were at the end of a short passageway, tucked away in an alcove. Paladin looked upwards, listened. Then he aimed high and fired a single shot. In the confines of that narrow passageway the detonation was deafening. Without waiting for the reverberations to fade, he ran up the stairs.

Most of the doors and whole sections of the walls had been destroyed by the fire. In those yawning, open spaces thus created, sound carried. As Paladin clattered upwards he could hear the thump of Corrigan's boots hammering up the main staircase. Rodriguez was up there waiting. He would hear two men, but if he'd listened to Corrigan his six-gun would be pointed at the dark opening of the back stairs.

If luck's on my side, Paladin thought wildly, *Corrigan's long legs will carry him up faster and he'll shoot the Mexican in the back before he blows me back down these stairs. And if I make sure that happens by slowing down now I can make damn sure of living to see another day. . . .*

Gritting his teeth he dumped that cowardly notion where it belonged, took the last few steps at breakneck speed and exploded out on to the first-floor landing.

It was wide, flooded with light from the big window. The sun was a golden orb about to drop behind the tall trees. Its glare was dazzling. Then that glare was matched by the flame from the muzzle of a six-gun. Guillermo Rodriguez was a black, silhouetted shape. He had placed himself in front of the window. To look at that slim form was to look directly into the setting sun's glare.

The shot cracked, echoed from the smoke-blackened walls. Seemingly without separation it was followed by a second. At the top of the main staircase, Brad Corrigan reeled to the side. One hand grabbed for the ornate bannisters. The other was clapped to his chest. Then his legs buckled. He fell backwards, hitting the stairs with his shoulders. Out of sight, the splintering thunder of his fall was sickening.

God damn that Mex, Paladin thought, *he wasn't for one second taken in by Corrigan's shouted warning about back stairs.*

Teeth bared, the marshal's fall a fading echo in his ears, Paladin fired three blind shots into the window's dazzling glare. At the black shape. At Guillermo Rodriguez.

But Rodriguez had gone.

In the fleeting second when Paladin had flashed a sideways glance at the falling marshal, the Mexican had slipped away up the next flight of stairs. Paladin was faced with another climb. This time he was on his own. He would be stepping out on to another blackened landing, but looking into the yawning muzzle of the same deadly six-gun.

A ghostly voice, feeble but clearly coming from a man far from dead, drifted up the stair well.

'Why do trapped men always flee upwards?' And then Brad Corrigan laughed hoarsely, the sound rasping across bare walls. 'I'm living proof that Mexican's a born loser with nowhere to hide, Paladin. Go get the sonofabitch.'

Relief flooded through Paladin, but the marshal's shouted encouragement did nothing to quell his fears. If there was a man with nowhere to hide, it was not Rodriguez. To reach him, Paladin had to climb the wide, open staircase. If he made it in one piece, he had no idea of the layout of the upper floor. He would again be exposed, walking naked into the unknown.

Did he have a choice?

It was true that the longer Rodriguez waited the more the tension would rise, the more the Mexican's nerves would fray, and frayed nerves led to fatal mistakes. But Paladin knew that if he put off going up that final staircase for too long, his nerve would break. He would turn tail, walk away. Rodriguez would have won without firing another shot – and that could not be allowed to happen.

So the only question was did he creep up step by step in a stealthy approach, or launch a desperate storming assault into a deadly hail of bullets?

Paladin shook his head irritably. He took a deep, shaky breath, reloaded his Colt, cocked the weapon. Then he squeezed his eyes shut, opened them again and hit the stairs at a run. His boots pounded on the bare wood. The double-back halfway up slowed him and he used a stiff left arm to push himself away from the wall and around the bend. Above him a blaze of light from the setting sun was flooding through the front window. He reached the second-floor landing in one final, breathless bound and flung himself bodily to one side. Expecting a bullet he would never hear to rip through his chest, his back, he rolled. He finished up with his back against a wall. His six-gun was up, levelled, seeking out the Mexican.

The landing was bathed in evening light.

It was empty.

Paladin banged his head back against the wall in frustration, touched his damp forehead with the six-gun's foresight, took a moment to settle his ragged breathing. Then he used a hand for leverage and sprang to his feet.

Footprints in the soot coating the floor led from the stairs to the French windows from which all glass had been exploded by the fire. Paladin rushed through them and out on to the balcony. He grabbed the rail and craned out precariously. He was in time to see Rodriguez hang by his fingertips from the lower balcony, then drop to the lawn.

The Mexican hit the grass hard, staggered, then regained his balance. Paladin fired at the running figure once, twice, but missed; a man shooting at a depressed angle must always aim deliberately low. Paladin had been too hasty; both his shots had screamed over the Mexican's head.

Rodriguez was lithe and fleet of foot. He ran for the side of the house. His horse would be hitched in the stable yard. Certain that he had done his job and meted out rough justice on the man who killed his mother, he would cross the Bowman-Laing bridge and ride flat out for Texas.

And Paladin's horse was tied to a tree a good hundred yards away.

'Damn it to hell,' Paladin swore, and quickly weighed his options. Wait for Rodriguez to come riding around from the stables, and try to shoot him out of the saddle? Or run for his own horse now and be ready to give chase?

The shot was too risky. Paladin spun and tore back into the house. He hammered down the stairs two at a time. Corrigan was on the first landing, shoulder bloody, sitting against the wall with his legs outstretched. He grinned weakly, flapped a hand. Paladin rushed by and continued on down, pushing hard off the walls at the turns. He pounded along the echoing hall and clattered down the steps. Rodriguez came tearing around the corner and on to the grass. Clods of dark earth flew from the hoofs of his racing horse. The Mexican's colourful sombrero was flying from its neck cord. His bared teeth were white in the now fading light.

Again Paladin tried to down the man. He stood with braced legs, holding the Colt .45 in both hands. But now he was faced with a fast-moving target. He fired twice. Both shots missed the fleeing Mexican, hissing into the tall trees. At the next squeeze of the trigger the hammer clicked on on a spent cartridge.

Swearing coarsely, then wisely curbing his fury to save breath, Paladin began to run.

He was no more than halfway to the trees where his horse was tethered when he heard a terrible tearing and splintering of wood. It was followed by a loud, fearful yell, and a huge splash.

The damn bridge has gone, Paladin thought wildly. He broke into a flat-out sprint. When he reached his horse it was straining back against the tether, ears pricked, eyes showing their whites. Paladin said something soothing. Then he dragged his Winchester from its saddle-boot and ran for the creek.

The sun had almost gone. The encircling stands of tall trees cast long shadows. Rodriguez's horse was thrusting itself back up the steep bank, rippling muscles streaming water. It made the top, stood trembling, stirrups swinging loosely. Paladin touched the wet horse, strode to the timber steps leading on to the Bowman-Laing bridge.

But there was no bridge.

It had collapsed under the weight of Rodriguez's horse. The Mexican had taken it too fast. He had reached halfway. Then one of his horse's hoofs had broken through a rotten board. Rodriguez had gone down with his horse into deep water. The splintered remains of the ancient creek crossing hung from both banks, the jagged ends of broken timber trailing in the water.

Rodriguez was clinging desperately to a thin, overhanging branch. His knuckles were white. The current was not strong, but he was some way out from the bank and out of his depth. The thin branch could not support his weight. Every now and then he went under. When he surfaced his sleek black hair was flattened to his head. His eyes were wild, staring, but when he spoke his voice was without fear.

'I cannot swim,' he said.

'I had your bullet in my back all those years ago when you dumped me in the Red. Swimming was difficult.'

'But you are here now and so I ask you—'

'Corrigan's alive.'

'*No es importante,* I—'

The branch dipped and he went under again. This time when he surfaced his nostrils were flared and there was a distant look in his eyes. Inside his clenched, white-knuckled fist the bark was stripping from the green branch.

'*Por favor,*' he said without emotion. '*Por favor,* Señor Paladin. . . .'

Paladin dropped the rifle and stepped carefully down the slippery bank. He pulled his folding knife from his pocket. The way he was turned, the knife was hidden from Rodriguez. Paladin thumbed open the blade. He looked down at the cold steel. He closed his eyes for an instant, swallowed the choking feeling in his throat; listened to the rushing of the water, the liquid sounds of a man drowning in silent stoicism.

Then he opened his eyes, bent down and with a single stroke of the razor-sharp blade he severed the taut branch.